RIFLES ON THE RIVER

NOEL M. LOOMIS

SAGEBRUSH
Large Print Westerns

First published in Great Britain by Collins
First published in the United States by Fawcett Gold Medal

First Isis Edition
published 2018
by arrangement with
Golden West Literary Agency

A catalogue record for this book is available
from the British Library.

ISBN 978–1–78541–546–3 (pb)

Published by
F. A. Thorpe (Publishing)
Anstey, Leicestershire

Set by Words & Graphics Ltd.
Anstey, Leicestershire
Printed and bound in Great Britain by
T. J. International Ltd., Padstow, Cornwall

This book is printed on acid-free paper

CHAPTER
ONE

It was June, 1773. The weather was hot and humid, and Dan Shankle studied the vast stretches of swamp as the canoes travelled against the brown water.

"Sure looks like agy bottoms to me," he called back.

"It's full of fever," Simon Jeffreys agreed from the second boat.

They had turned off from the Mississippi and the Choctaws had paddled the big canoes up the wide bends of the Arkansa River, through a heavy, oppressive atmosphere that made the sweat run in streams down their copper skins.

Dan had not failed to note that the Choctaws, who had been full of nasal talk as they started out that morning, had lost their loquaciousness as they ascended the river; they were watchful and silent as they progressed towards Osage country. It was a relief to hear one of them aspirate the word for heat:

"*Lashpa!*"

Dan continued to search the shore on both sides as far ahead as he could see. "It'll get hotter when summer comes," he said.

Simon growled from behind. "If it gets any worse than this, I say let the Quapaws keep it. A man can't make an honest shilling in this kind of weather."

Dan turned back to keep his lookout. When Indians were nervous, no white man but a fool would fail to keep his eye peeled.

Kneeling in the bow, he was tall and singularly thin, but he seemed to fill the fringed buckskin hunting-shirt rather well, and the hair that showed long from under his coon-skin cap was light brown except where the ends were bleached by the sun.

All the morning they had travelled through a heavy inundated forest of tall cypress with thick, buttressed trunks, and of tupelo gum with pendulous clusters of olive-like fruits not yet turning purple. There were frequent breaks in the river banks, and the brown water poured through them into lakes and bayous and vast cypress swamps, so that they needed a careful watch to keep the channel.

From just ahead came the heavy splash of an alligator launching itself into the river and a water moccasin, hardly visible as it lay stretched along the tentacle-like grey root of a cypress tree, slid into the water as they went by.

"*Nampa*," said one of the Indians behind Dan, and there was a chorus of grunts.

Dan held out his hand as a signal to the Choctaws to stop paddling. The twenty-foot canoe with its two thousand pounds of goods lost headway and the second canoe came alongside.

Dan looked at Simon Jeffreys. They were dressed about alike, but Simon was shorter and darker and a little fat.

"How much farther to Arkansa Post?" said Dan.

"Can't be far . . . three or four leagues."

"You've been in Louisiana so long you think like a Spaniard," said Dan.

"You'll learn it soon enough," Simon said sourly. "Your first lesson is up ahead."

The Choctaws started to paddle again and the canoes moved upstream side by side. Presently the Indian who had spoken before said in a low voice, "*Holihta kallo.*"

"What's that mean?" asked Dan.

"A fort," said Simon. "Up ahead there — Arkansa Post."

Dan had to look carefully for the cabins, built of weather-worn cypress and thatched with grass and leaves, blended so closely into the background as to be easily missed.

Four small cabins and a palisaded larger cabin marked the seat of government in the Arkansa country, the only law between St. Louis and Natchitoches. A dog barked at the canoes, and a Mexican in a big straw peon hat woke up slowly from his siesta in the shade of a thick stand of birch trees. He stared for a moment. Then he scurried to the large cabin while Dan's canoe slid to a stop with its bow high on the clay.

Dan jumped out and pulled the bow a few inches higher. The Choctaws, impassive, watched with glittering eyes. Simon's boat slid up and Dan pulled it beside the first.

Simon said, "Comp'ny's comin'. And not good comp'ny."

"Trouble?" Dan asked, pushing his powder-horn back to his side.

"His coat is lined with light blue. He's a lieutenant of hussars."

"Is that worse than cavalry?"

Simon said uncomfortably, "Don't under-rate this gent. He represents the King of Spain. Don't keep your back towards him."

Dan turned slowly. The black-haired Spaniard was a young, handsome man, filled with the animal vigour of youth and the arrogance of a Spanish official.

He was flanked by four Spanish soldiers, black-haired, bright-eyed, and bearing flintlock muskets. The officer was impeccably dressed, but the soldiers were not. To judge from the red feathers in their hats, they were infantrymen, but their uniforms were sloppy. One wore moccasins; a second had no powder-horn; and a third had no blunderbuss in his belt.

The Spaniards stopped six feet from him. "*¿Quién es V., señor?*"

"I'm Dan Shankle, an Englishman. These are my men."

"Your home, señor?"

"Wyoming Valley, Pennsylvania."

The officer's eyes narrowed slightly. "Your business?"

Dan motioned towards the boats behind him without taking his eyes from the Spaniard. "I came to trade."

4

"Your passport?"

Dan shook his head sadly. "I did not know a passport would be required on the Arkansa."

"A passport is required of all foreigners in New Spain, particularly of Englishmen," the officer said stiffly.

"Are you the commandant here?"

"I represent Don Fernando de Leyva, commandant of this district, with full power to discharge his duties."

"We aren't looking for trouble," Dan said.

"You have trade goods, no?"

Dan nodded.

"May I see your licence to trade?"

"I didn't know . . ."

The officer said sharply, "You know very little, *señor*. May I ask with whom you expect to trade in the Arkansa country?"

"Indians."

"What tribe of Indians?"

Dan shrugged. "Any kind."

The officer considered. "Since you are so ignorant of His Most Catholic Majesty's regulations, perhaps you have brought some nice rifles to trade to the Osages? *¿Verdad?*"

Dan shook his head.

"You have a rifle in the bow of your boat, *señor*."

"For my own use." Dan nodded towards Simon. "He has one too. Beyond that we have none."

"You have knives, undoubtedly."

Dan nodded. "One apiece."

5

The black eyes drilled into him. "But none in your goods?"

Dan met his stare. "None."

"The law is the law," the officer said implacably.

Dan tried to look apologetic. "We aren't aiming to violate the law. We just come to do some harmless trading."

"You will submit to inspection of your cargo?"

"Sure," Dan said negligently. "Help yourself. If I've got something that shouldn't be there, you can keep it." Without taking his gaze from Dan's face, the officer barked an unmilitary command: "¡Vayan!" The four soldiers slouched away unconcerned.

Dan allowed himself a deeper breath. So far it was going according to schedule.

"I will inspect your cargo," the officer said; "but I warn you that firearms will not be admitted."

Dan was a little relieved. The very fact that his goods would be examined, though he was without a passport or a trading licence, indicated that Simon had known what he was talking about. "I understand the English are working out of the Illinois country, trading rifles to the Osages."

The officer looked sharply at him. "That is true. Farther up the river the Osages are well supplied, and we have not enough force in this post to stop it."

"The Osages are out of your territory anyway, aren't they?"

The officer shrugged. "It is an involved affair. The Osages travel to the Red River of Natchitoches, half-way between here and Santa Fé, and raid the

Taovayas or Wichitas. The Wichitas in turn demand more firearms from the authorities in Béxar."

"Why not let them have them?"

The officer sighed. "It is not as simple as that. The Wichitas trade firearms to the savage Cayugas and Camanches and these in turn raid the Spanish settlements to the great displeasure of the Viceroy. If the Camanches had access to plenty of gunpowder and rifles, the Spanish in Tejas would be wiped out."

"Then it is good that rifles are not permitted up the Arkansa."

The officer looked at him sharply. "What city have you sailed from?"

"Baltimore."

"Arkansa is a long way from Baltimore. It is a vicious country, very wild and primitive," the officer explained. "The Osages are *muy malos indios.*"

"I've been fighting Indians all my life."

The officer shrugged. "Now," said he, "shall we inspect your cargo?"

Dan knew they were only sparring — *platicando,* Simon had called it, warning him that it was a part of the Spanish way of life. "At your leisure," he said, turning to the boats.

Simon and his Indians were unfastening the canvas in the second canoe. The officer ran an eye over its contents while they held the canvas up at one side. His sharp black eyes scanned the contents. "Beads, cloth, vermilion, looking-glasses . . . the usual goods," he noted, and turned away.

Simon, impassive, dropped the canvas and motioned the Choctaws to refasten it at the back, while he bent down at the front.

The Spaniard turned to Dan's boat. Dan hastened to lift the canvas. The Spaniard's quick eyes took in everything. "No rifles?" he asked, looking at Dan.

"No rifles."

"No knives?"

Dan shook his head.

"Gunpowder?"

"Only enough for our own use."

"What's in the small buckskin bag there on top?"

Dan stared. "I don't know," he said slowly. "I've never seen it before."

"Very curious," the officer said, but did not take his eyes from the bag.

"You'd better examine it."

Dan saw the bright gleam of avarice in the Spaniard's eyes as he leaned over and lifted the bag. "It's quite heavy."

Dan cut the rawhide string with his knife. The bag opened up and lay in the Spaniard's hand. He glanced up at Dan. "*Reales*, pieces of eight," he said.

"Are they of legal coinage?"

"They appear so," the Spaniard said.

"I make out about forty of them."

"Part of your trade goods, no doubt?"

Dan looked up, wide-eyed. "I never saw them before," he said.

"A strange thing, indeed!" But the Spaniard did not seem astonished.

"Strange enough . . . but, since they are not mine, perhaps it would be proper for you to keep them for the rightful owner, while I take my outfit on up the river."

The Spaniard weighed the bag in his hand. Then he stepped back. "Very well. I suggest you get far enough up the river to avoid interference with my men. *Buenos dias, señor.*"

Dan nodded and jerked his head at Simon, who was now standing at the bow of the second canoe.

"Push off," he said tersely. He braced his legs, lifted the bow of the second canoe, and gave it a powerful shove. He followed it into the water and leaped into the bow. The Choctaws were paddling, and the big canoe began to move upstream. Dan glanced back. Simon was following. Neither of them looked towards the fort.

CHAPTER
TWO

They rounded a bend, where a stand of cypress trees along the edge of the brown water cut them off from the sight of Arkansa Post. Dan took a deep breath and motioned the Choctaws to hold up paddling until Simon came alongside.

"For a minute," he said, "I thought he wasn't going to take it."

Simon's lips twisted scornfully. "They always take it — if it's enough. The Spanish colonial policy would strangle the life out of every settlement in New Spain if the officials didn't allow contraband through. In the first place, the duties are so heavy that they make legal goods cost two or three times what they should. In the second place, Spain is not an industrial country. If all the goods not needed in Spain could be shipped over here, the settlers would still be hungry for stuff. They've got to have English and French and Dutch goods or they can't live. You should see some of the colonists who have been up around Santa Fé, or down around Béxar, for fifteen or twenty years. Unless they're rich, they live like animals; they have almost nothing but food and shelter."

"Then they really *need* contraband?"

"They've got to have it, and some officials are financing the *contrabandistas*."

"Up here on the Arkansa?"

"I don't know about this, but they sure are down along the rivers in the New Philippines, or Tejas country, whatever they call it."

"Are we through with Arkansa Post?" asked Dan.

Simon bit off a chew. "I think so. The only thing that worried the lieutenant was that you might be a spy for Unzaga. You look too honest to be a *contrabandista*."

"Good thing I ran across you in New Orleans; otherwise I'd have tried to go through Natchitoches."

"That way you'd have been tied up, for de Mézières is one official who can't be bought. Without a passport you'd have been sent back; *with* a passport you'd be tied hand and foot because you'd have to conform to all the regulations." He put the tobacco in his shirt. "If you've got to trade with the Indians, this is the way to do it. Provided you get past the post, and don't rub the fur of the *contrabandistas* the wrong way, you can trade as you please, come and go as you like, and answer to nobody. By the way," he said, being so casual that it was obvious, "you never did tell me what you came down here for?" He watched the stream ahead. "You didn't come all the way to Arkansa just to trade glass beads to the Indians."

Dan took a deep breath, but did not answer.

"There's two more hills to climb," said Simon finally. "The *contrabandistas* and the Osages."

"What about the *contrabandistas*?"

"They're the worst bunch of outlaws in Louisiana."

"How do they get rid of the slaves and horses they get from the Indians?"

"Run them down to Little Manchac if they're in a hurry, the place where you bought your stuff. More goods go through Little Manchac than through New Orleans, and every bead is contraband. If they're not in a hurry, they wait for a licensed trader to come up from New Orleans."

"How does he get around the regulations?"

"He isn't trading with Indians," said Simon.

A grunt came from one of the Choctaws.

"*Hatak panshi*," said another.

More grunts.

"What are they talking about?" asked Dan.

"Scalps," said Simon.

Dan looked around. "What scalps?"

Simon dropped into the nasal language of the Indians, "*Himmona?*"

Heads nodded vigorously in both boats.

"Fresh scalps," Simon said laconically. "Osage, by the look of them."

They were now almost even with a dilapidated cabin, around which the only sign of habitation consisted of three black-haired scalp-locks hanging on wooden pegs driven between the logs.

"Probably a *contrabandista* lives there," said Simon.

"The Choctaws don't like it," Dan observed.

"No. It means there'll be Osages looking for hair to even things up."

"I thought," said Dan, "the Spanish had the Indians under control."

"How could they, with ten or twelve soldiers at Arkansa Post to control thousands of Indians? For ninety years the only good of this post is as a place for the Quapaws to come for their presents."

"How about the Osages?"

"They get their presents in St. Louis and their rifles from the English."

Three leagues upstream from the post they were still surrounded by swamp, dormant lakes, and stagnant bayous, covering mile after mile. "How much farther?" asked Dan.

Simon scowled. "We should be gettin' there. You in a hurry to get it over with?"

Dan realised he was tense. "Like to know where I stand."

"You'll find out soon. That's it, up ahead."

Through the trees Dan saw a blockhouse, bigger and stronger than the fort. "It looks business-like," he said.

"Is is El Cadrón, headquarters for all the *contrabandista* trade."

"The Spanish know about it?"

"They don't bother it. El Cadrón makes the Post of Arkansa worth a lot of money, and it also keeps the Osages away from the post."

Dan pointed with the paddle. The Choctaws turned the canoe into a small bay formed by a bend of the river. A sandbar ran across it, and on this grew a thick stand of young cottonwoods.

"Try around the end," said Simon. "It looks like enough water on the other side of the bar. Anyway, I can see boat marks through the *álamos*."

There were two feet of water beyond the bar. Dan led the way into the protected strip, and the bow of the canoe crunched on sand. Dan got out. "Who built the blockhouse?" he asked.

"The British built it, and they bring most of the goods up here. Frenchmen do most of the trading with the Indians."

Dan pulled up the bow and turned to look at the blockhouse. It was considerably bigger than the fort at Arkansa Post, and had about the same group of smaller log cabins around it. Two black-haired Indian squaws with copper bands on their upper arms were scraping a fresh bearskin on the ground in front of the blockhouse, while two red-capped *voyageurs* sat on the ground, one at each side of the door, leaning against the logs and smoking pipes. One called out a name that Dan did not hear clearly.

He heard the obble-obble-obble of wild turkeys from across the river, and turned that way for a moment. Creeping through a thicket of wild plum trees, protected from sight of the turkeys by a slight rise in the ground, were three naked Indian or half-breed boys with small bows and arrows.

The second canoe gritted on the sand and Dan pulled it up. He looked back at the doorway of the blockhouse as Simon Jeffreys stepped out of the canoe. A huge man was in the doorway. He squinted at the boats and then slowly, deliberately, and insolently came down to meet them, while two men who appeared to be Frenchmen got up from beside the door and fell in behind him.

14

One of the Frenchmen was tall and concave-stomached; the other was short, square-framed and filled with energy. All three, like Dan and Simon, were dressed in frontier garb: long buckskin hunting-shirt fastened with a wide leather belt; six-inch fringes hanging from the sleeves; the lower or skirt portions black and greasy from long use. Each had a pistol in his belt; all had knives on their right hips, and the giant had a brass tomahawk on his left hip. They wore Indian moccasins and long buckskin leggings; the giant wore a shapeless, big-brimmed, buffalo-wool hat; the two Frenchmen following him wore red stocking caps.

"Watch out," Simon warned in a low voice.

Dan took a deep breath. "There won't be much choice here."

Simon shook his head.

The squaws, still squatting over the bearskin, had stopped their work and were watching. Dan stood between the two boats. Abruptly most of the noises of the wilderness seemed to cease, and there was left only the erratic gobble of the turkeys.

Dan glanced around. The Choctaw paddlers were sitting quietly, impassive, their black eyes fixed on the three approaching men. The turkeys were still gobbling as they fed on the mast under the oak. The three men stopped about six feet from Dan. The big man was rough in the face and wild-eyed; his black hair was uncombed; his face was toughened by wind and sun, his nose aquiline.

"Where you from?" His voice was filled with suspicion.

Dan said, "Down the river."

"What's in the boats?"

"Goods from Little Manchac."

The giant stared. "Who'd you buy 'em from?"

"An English trader."

"How'd you get by Arkansa Post?"

"The lieutenant inspected my cargo and found a small bag of gold that didn't belong to me."

"You got too many answers. You're a liar!"

Dan's temper began to rise, but he kept his tongue.

"Pull out of here! ordered the big man.

Dan looked at him without change of expression. He pulled out his carrot of tobacco and bit off a chew, taking his time. "Unload!" he said to the Indians.

The big man strode forward ominously. "Not here," he said harshly.

The Choctaws did not move.

"Why not here?" asked Dan.

"I got goods to sell. If you want to buy, you can unload here. If you got your own stuff, go on up the river and take your chances with the Osages."

"That's maybe a good idea," Dan said slowly. "I never liked a fellow who thought he owned the country, anyway."

The big man's eyes were flinty, but he didn't answer.

"Simon," said Dan without turning, "push off your boat."

"I can push it off," said Simon, but for the first time he sounded dubious. "You're gonna have trouble with the crew, though."

Dan glanced quickly at the Choctaws. Their faces were blank, but all were shaking their heads. "Why?" asked Dan. "What's the matter with them?"

16

"Scalps," said Simon.

"Whose?"

"Their own."

"You mean they're afraid of the Osages?"

Simon nodded. "It's mid-afternoon and they want to get back out of the Arkansa country before dark. They don't like the mosquitoes up here."

"I don't seem to have any choice."

"Not much," said Simon.

"All right, we'll unload here. Tear off that canvas!"

"Hold on a minute, mister!" The big man moved two steps closer. "There's only one way you can unload here: if you was sent by the right man. And if you was, you better sing out."

Dan paused. He tried to remember the name of the man from whom he had bought the goods in Little Manchac, the smuggling port for Tejas. He looked at Simon for help. Simon hesitated for an instant and then said, "Clermont." He sounded sure of himself, but Dan, watching his eyes, knew it was a gamble.

Dan looked at the big man and nodded. He saw the big man was taken aback, and for a moment Dan thought it was a wild guess that had hit dead centre.

But the big man gathered his wits. "Who was with Clermont?"

Simon answered promptly, "Poeyfarré."

Dan looked at the big man, and what he saw was no good.

The big man was grinning. "You mighta said Harry Blundin, and you woulda been wrong, because I'm Harry Blundin. You mighta said Duvivier, because

17

Duvivier is with Clermont this summer, buyin' horses and mules from the Lipan Apaches to sell to the English colonies when the war starts. But you said Poeyfarré . . . and this is Poeyfarré behind me."

Dan felt his muscles begin to loosen up. He didn't have time to ask, "What war?" because Blundin grabbed him.

The big man was three inches taller and twice as thick in the body. They strained at each other, Blundin trying to break him over backward. Dan was lithe but he was tough. He gave a little and then he got his fingers in the man's eyes and nose and pushed him back hard.

Dan circled. The two Frenchmen were watching coldly. The Indian squaws had come from their work on the bearskin and were standing, barefooted, watching without expression. These things Dan Shankle saw as he circled to the right. Simon was still on his knees in the boat and the bronze faces of the Choctaws were as impassive as the broad faces of the Osage squaws. There was no sound above the hum of insect life save for the sudden gobble of a turkey under the oak tree across the river. Then Blundin lunged.

After the first encounter they circled each other warily. Blood dripped from Dan's nose. Blundin's eyes were burning with fury, but he was cautious. He had sampled the man from Pennsylvania and had found he might have more trouble than he had anticipated.

In the next encounter Dan made the first rush. He lowered his head and rammed his skull against the pit of the man's stomach.

18

Blundin grunted and staggered. He fell back and pulled Dan with him. He got his big legs under Dan and straightened them out like a crossbow released. Dan felt himself lifted free and catapulted into the air. Then he was falling into the water between his two canoes, on his back, spreadeagled, while Blundin came thundering after him.

In the water Dan had the advantage. He could swim.

Blundin threshed like a drowning buffalo, but Dan held him under the water. Then he looked around. They were almost under the cliff where the turkeys had been. He gave Blundin a push towards shore. He pulled up in the mud under the overhanging brush. He got Blundin by the hair and held him out in the stream, nose above water. The big man began to splutter and struggle.

"Be quiet," Dan said, "or I'll drown you." He pushed his head under the water and brought it back.

Dan pulled the man towards the bank by the hair, and with his feet pushed out into the stream. He swam across to the sloping sand shore, and walked out dripping wet. He advanced on Poeyfarré and the other Frenchman. "Have either of you gents got anything to say?"

Poeyfarré's face didn't change. His eyes were small and watchful. Finally he said, "I have notheeng to say," and his arms hung straight at his sides.

Dan turned to the lanky one. "Satisfied?" asked Dan.

The man nodded quietly. "I'm Chamillard. I am satisfied."

Dan glanced at the squaws. They were chattering excitedly and giggling, watching Blundin climb the opposite bank. At Dan's stare they quieted suddenly, watching him with big dark eyes, alert, suspicious. They were both young, and looked good to a man who had been away from women for a long time. Perversely, it made him want to hurt them.

"You've got no loyalty!" he said scathingly.

They stared at him without a change of expression. Behind him Chamillard said coldly, "Why should they have? He bought them both for one rifle, and in a couple of months he'll get tired of them and sell them down the river as slaves . . . if he doesn't get mad and kill them first."

Dan turned slowly. "Simon!"

"Here," said Simon from a seat on a cypress root.

"Tell the Choctaws to unload the canoes and . . ."

"The Choctaws have already unloaded the stove-in one, and I let them have it."

"What for?"

"Choctaws are funny cusses," Simon observed, and pulled out his carrot of tobacco. He began to size it up for a chew. "They like to keep their hair. They figgered to get out of Osage country before dark, and I agreed with 'em. For a couple of escudos I'da gone with 'em." Simon looked up, and it astonished Dan to see that there was a worried air about him.

Dan looked at the pile of goods on the sand, covered by canvas. He'd been too intent on the two Frenchmen to see anything else. Now he took a long breath. "You should of had them carry it higher," he said.

CHAPTER
THREE

Poeyfarré and Chamillard went back towards the blockhouse. Across the river, Blundin was following the bank to where a small canoe was tied.

Dan turned to the canoe. The squaws had gone back to their bearskin and now were squatted on each side of it, scraping away the surplus flesh with chisel-shaped bones and watching him covertly as they talked Osage in low voices.

"Where do you figure to unload?" asked Simon.

Dan sized up the sandy beach. "We'll pull up to that first bunch of willows. There's high ground behind them in case of a rise in the river."

They spent an hour moving the canoe to the new spot, and then carrying the already unloaded goods to the willow trees. While they were at it, Blundin came across the river in the small canoe, and pushed it back into the water.

Dan saw three naked Indian children standing at the top of the bank watching. They'd get their boat, all right, although they'd have to wait for the stream to bring it to them. Blundin went to the blockhouse without looking at Simon or Dan.

"You might have more trouble with him," said Simon.

"We won't be here that long."

They piled the goods and covered it with canvas. Simon built a fire with flint and steel, striking it into some charred cloth that he kept in a hollow joint of cane. Dan opened a meal gum, dipped out a double handful of corn meal with a gourd, filled it up with river water, and stirred it with his knife. He put in another small handful of meal to thicken it, while Simon cut some slabs of fat pork. Dan set the gourd of cornmeal down by the fire.

"Make up some ash cakes," he said, "and I'll order some meat."

Simon laid the white strips of salt pork in the skillet. They sizzled when they touched the hot iron.

Dan was going back to the sandy beach where they had first landed. The small canoe, paddled by three naked Indian or half-breed boys whose eyes looked white and big in their coppery faces, was pulling around the upper end of the sandbar. They quit paddling as they got into quiet water, and watched Dan. He held out a string of blue and red beads, pointing at their boat. They shook their heads solemnly, holding up their paddles so that the boat floated half-way between the sandbar and the beach. Dan held a string of red and blue and green glass beads; then he pointed at them, and said, "Obble . . . obble . . . obble."

The biggest boy watched the beads. He dug his paddle into the water and brought the canoe into shore. He held up a fat turkey-cock by its neck. Dan took the turkey by the neck and gave the beads to the boy, then waited for his approval or disapproval. The boy grabbed the beads and ran off towards the blockhouse.

Dan returned to the fire beyond the willows. Simon's back was towards him as he shaped cornmeal cakes and dropped them into the greased skillet.

Dan used a strip of rawhide to tie the bird to a tree, and began to skin it.

Simon was watching him curiously. "You get along all right," he noted. "You're a fooler in a fight, and you know your business, but just what are you doing in the Arkansa country?"

"No mystery about that," said Dan. "You've known me all your life. We grew up together, didn't we?"

"Sure . . . and when we ran into each other on the levee that day you got in on the Philadelphia boat, right off you said you wanted to go up the Arkansa to do some trading."

"That's where we are, isn't it?"

Simon used the skillet to level out a place in the ashes. "What I'd like to know is how you were so sure you wanted to come up here."

Dan heard voices and looked up. Half a dozen red-capped men were emerging from the forest beyond the blockhouse, following a well-worn trail. They turned into the blockhouse, past the squaws, and Dan finished pushing clay-covered pieces of turkey into the ashes.

"I never asked if you had a passport," said Simon, "because if you had had one you'd of gone to Natchitoches."

Dan looked at him across the fire. "I'm looking for a man — a man who is somehow diverting rifles from the frontier in Pennsylvania to the Indians in the Tejas country."

Simon looked sceptical. "How can you make any money at that?"

"I won't," said Dan; "but I may save some lives." He stood up. "Ash cake and turkey," he said. "I wish we had something different for a change."

"Yesterday," said Simon, eyeing him from where he squatted before the fire, "you had catfish. The day before you had buffalo; the day before that it was panther; the day before that it was alligator tail." He scratched his whiskers. "Maybe I'm not no gourmet, but it seems to me you've had a well-set table."

"Meat!" said Dan. "I'd give a shilling for a dozen eggs."

"You would?" Simon got up. "I'll be back."

Dan wasn't watching him. He had his eye on the six or seven men who had come out of the woods. All had gone into the blockhouse but one, who was palavering with the squaws. Dan glanced at Simon's broad back as he walked down the sandy shore. Then he stared back at the fire.

The Frenchman finished his discussion with the squaws, and both of them showed him their beads. Apparently they had divided. The Frenchman looked up at Dan and went into the blockhouse. The squaws kept chipping away at the bearskin. Smoke began to pour out of the blockhouse chimney, and a roar came from the door. Both squaws got hastily to their feet and went to the blockhouse. Dan guessed the Frenchmen were ready to eat.

Simon came back and held out his coon-skin cap. "Two shillings' worth," he said.

Dan stared. The cap was filled with what looked like eggs, all right, but they were about half the size of a hen's egg and they were round. He picked one up and almost dropped it, for the shell wasn't hard like a hen's egg, but leathery and tough. He rolled it around in his fingers. "What laid it?"

"A turtle. They lay them in the sand and cover them."

"They're probably not very fresh."

"For a shilling a dozen you can't afford to be finical."

"How do you cook them?"

"You can fry 'em," said Simon; "but I don't recommend it." He broke the shell with his knife point and let it run out into his hand, then held it towards Dan.

Dan sniffed. "It stinks!" he said.

"They eat better than they smell. I'll get some of that clay and we'll roast 'em."

They coated the turtle eggs and dropped them into the hot ashes. They sat back then, Dan against a big cottonwood tree that was just beginning to release cottony puffs that floated everywhere in the air, and Simon against a black willow tree whose foot-thick trunk showed a ripe old age. Both pulled out their tobacco and looked for a place to take the next chew.

Simon put his carrot back into his shirt. "There's still some things make me wonder," he observed.

Dan watched the fire. "What are they?"

"You got by Arkansa Post too easy, for one thing."

"I did just what you told me to do."

"I know — but it went mighty slick, if you ask me."

"What else?"

"You came in here and camped in the front yard of the *contrabandistas* like you owned the place — and this is the toughest bunch of outlaws in all the Spanish colonies."

Dan chewed his tobacco. "Anything else?"

"Yeah. You didn't bring whisky or rifles — just four thousand pounds of ordinary trade goods, which you could as well of taken through Natchitoches."

"You told me yourself," said Dan, "a man can't accept anything but skins from the Indians if he goes back through Natchitoches."

Simon nodded. His right jaw was bulging from the chew. "All that is true enough. If a man wants to trade for horses and mules and slaves, he can't do it through de Mézières's country. But there's something almighty strange about this trip." He looked at the blockhouse. "If you really wanted that kind of goods, why didn't you bring rifles and gunpowder? How do you figure to compete with Blundin's men when you've got lookin'-glasses and beads?"

Dan didn't look up. The sun was now behind a ridge of woods in the west, and the rising hum of mosquitoes had reached a considerable volume. He got up and sliced off some green willow branches and threw them on the fire. Thick white smoke began to pour into the air.

"We're havin' more company," Simon said. "That second Frenchman is tired of bear-meat. Maybe *he* likes turtle eggs."

Dan went to the pile of goods and lifted one corner of the canvas. He put something into his shirt and dropped the canvas. Then he went back and sat down.

The lanky Frenchman sauntered towards their fire, wiping his knife-blade on his woollen pants. He stopped to face Dan, and dropped his knife in its sheath. "I'm Chamillard," he said.

"Have a seat. I'm Dan Shankle."

"*Merci*." Chamillard sat down against the cottonwood and pulled out a pipe.

"Try this," Dan said, withdrawing a full carrot of tobacco from his shirt.

The Frenchman looked up, studied Dan, and nodded as he took the tobacco. He shaved off trimmings with his knife and filled the bowl of the pipe. He snapped off a couple of green twigs and got a coal from the fire to light up. The smell was very pleasant.

Chamillard looked at him finally, when the pipe was emitting clouds of smoke. "You're a good man in a fight," he said, "and I like you ... *mais oui*. But maybe," he added coldly, "you're a spyspy for the Spanish, just as Blundin maintains."

Dan said with equal coldness, "I'm no spy for the Spanish."

Chamillard pondered this. "You look' for something special?"

A puff of tree-cotton was snuffed up against Dan's nose, and he batted at it as if it had been a mosquito. "What special, for instance?"

"It is a violent life along the Arkansa. I remember thirteen years ago when Brindamúr was killed."

"I never heard of Brindamúr."

Chamillard looked at him over the pipe. "You are quick to deny it," he noted. "Brindamúr, however, was killed in 1760 by a man named Morván. Morván was captured three years ago in an Indian village. No, I do not suspect anybody of seeking vengeance for Brindamúr. He was brutal and a tyrant . . . and no one on the Arkansa remembers a man thirteen years. I was merely using him as an idea, you might say. Sometimes men get killed, and sometimes their friends come hunting the killer. But the Arkansa is not a place for a man to hunt revenge. It is enough to stay alive without adding unnecessary complications."

Dan worked his chew. He got up and pushed a piece of turkey farther into the fire. Then he turned around. "I am not looking for revenge," he said. "I came to trade with the Indians."

"What Indians?"

Dan looked straight at him. "Any Indians. Just so I make a profit."

Chamillard's eyes dropped to his pipe. "You can go upstream a hundred leagues, into the Trois Rivières country, and trade with the Osages, but they get goods from the English, and so they drive a hard bargain."

Dan began to get a picture. "Where is it better?" he asked.

Chamillard watched him over the pipe. "A number of us are leaving in the morning for the Pani Piqué villages on the Rivière Rouge over in the Tejas country."

"Pani Piqué?"

"Wichita," said Simon.

"We can use some extra men to protect ourselves from the Osages." He paused. "We raided a band of Osages the last trip and got some scalps and two squaws. They'll be looking for us when we go back."

"I thought the Osage country was farther north."

"The Osages do not confine themselves to any given place," said Chamillard. "They are almost as bad as the Naytanes."

"He means Camanches," Simon said. "Every country has a different name for every tribe."

"The Osages don't like for us to trade with the Wichitas, for they are always on the warpath against the Wichitas and Camanches, and they know that we are the ones who furnish rifles to the Tejas tribes."

"The Osages don't like you, then?"

Chamillard shrugged and looked towards the blockhouse. "We kill them and take their squaws. It doesn't help."

"How are the Wichitas?"

"Indians, like all the rest, but not so dangerous. They raise pumpkins and squash, fight when they have to. They are usually at peace with the Camanches. An Indian peace, that is, with nobody trusting anybody else as far as you can kill a bull buffalo with a tomahawk."

"Why do they even pretend?"

"The Camanches get firearms and get rid of their stock and their slaves through the Wichitas. The Wichitas make a profit."

"The Wichitas ought to be happy."

"They complain about one thing: the licensed traders from Natchitoches don't bring them enough rifles and gunpowder to fight the Osages."

"So they do business with the *contrabandistas?*"

Chamillard nodded. "They have to."

"And the Camanches . . ."

"They raid the Spanish from Santa Fé to Chihuahua and Béxar; they raid the Apaches wherever they find them. They kill the men, but they keep the women and children and sell them to the Wichitas . . . and eventually they pass through Arkansa Post and end up in Louisiana." Chamillard blew a cloud of smoke into a swarm of mosquitoes.

"What about these two Osage squaws in camp now?"

"They're Blundin's. You could probably borrow one if you want."

"Have you got any idea where I can get mules to pack my goods?"

Chamillard knocked out his pipe. "See Blundin."

"After the fight we've just had?"

"Blundin's English. He's in business for a profit. He'll sell you mules if you can pay for them."

The turkey was tender and cooked through when Dan got back.

"You have any luck with him?" asked Simon.

"Some." Dan ripped the baked clay from a turkey thigh and bit into the juicy meat. "I got mules . . . at a price."

"How much of a price?"

Dan stripped the last meat from the bone and tossed it away. "I traded him half my stuff for twelve mules . . . enough to carry the other half and you and me."

Simon was fishing baked eggs out of the fire. "Pretty high price for mules, ain't it?"

"About $165 apiece."

"The best mule on earth isn't worth over a hundred."

"He is if you need him."

"You don't need 'em that bad. You've still got the canoe. We can go upriver a little ways and peddle the stuff to the Osages. You could get mules from them for about a fourth of what you paid."

Dan cracked open another piece of turkey. "As I understand it, these Wichita villages are the trading centre for all of Tejas."

"For the Norteños anyway."

"Who are they?"

"The northern tribes —Wichitas, Penateka Camanches, Kotsoteka Camanches, Pawnees, and some others."

"Then they are the people I want to do business with," said Dan. "The Norteños."

"You're sure a hard-headed cuss," said Simon. "Have a turtle egg."

CHAPTER
FOUR

They were up long before daylight. Chamillard and a man named Dartigo came to help them load the mules. Poeyfarré appeared to be the leader of the train. He would have twenty-two mules, and two men to help him with the mules, while the rest seemed to be more in the nature of guards.

They were under way by sun-up, striking from the blockhouse through the surrounding swamp, leaving the two squaws and their children behind, threading a twisting path among the cypress trees and the swamp grass and the water lilies, fighting off mosquitoes and botflies.

Along towards noon Poeyfarré stopped. "Unpack your mules," he told Dan. Poeyfarré was a big-faced man with a lantern jaw. "We'll let the mules graze until the middle of the afternoon. Then we'll move on. There's a safe place to camp about three leagues up the rivaire."

"When do we cross over?"

Poeyfarré stuck out his chin at Dan. "You ask questions," he said. "We cross in a couple of days, when the river gets shallow. *You* can cross any time."

Abruptly there was silence around them, and Dan felt the impact of suspicion and belligerence. He looked at Poeyfarré and said quietly, "I started with you. I'll finish with you."

Chamillard was building a fire while Dartigo and a man named Poupelinière were taking care of Poeyfarré's mules. Two other Frenchmen, Menard and Brognard, who had dropped out earlier, now came up with a gutted deer carcass, which they cut up and hung over the fire while they ate the liver raw.

That afternoon they followed a narrow ridge, with the river on the left and the swamps on the right. Occasionally they had to ford a shallow pass where the water had cut through at overflow time. But the swamps grew smaller as they progressed north-west. It was still humid and hot, but the nature of the country began to change. Pine trees began to appear on bluffs along the river, and a vast prairie extended for thirty leagues, but still, in the timbered bottoms, the air was close and stifling. The pines grew bigger and the oaks became more plentiful. There was red elm, yellow poplar, and blue ash, with slender persimmons on the higher ground, along with an occasional ornamental sassafras tree. They crossed the river but followed it. The country turned mountainous.

One morning they came across pony tracks that led up from the river and entered the trail from an open, grassy place. Menard, a slender, medium-height man with black hair, got down and examined the grass. "Ponies with riders," he said. "Most likely Indians.

Droppings still warm. They were here this morning —
maybe so two hours ago."

"How many?" Poeyfarré asked thoughtfully.

"Six ponies."

"Squaws?"

Menard back-tracked to the river bank, looked
around, and came back. "Squaws and bucks."

Poeyfarré's heavy jaw worked in thought. "With
squaws along, they aren't hunting trouble."

"They're headed north-west," Dartigo said. "They
must have started from the north-west or we'd have run
across their trail before."

Poeyfarré stared at him. "So?"

"So they know we're coming, and they've gone to tell
the main tribe."

Poeyfarré squinted at the sun. "They probably won't
get there before evening. By that time we'll be ready to
turn off the river."

The train was now headed west, but Chamillard kept
looking to the north-west. Dartigo, watching him, said
something in French, and Chamillard answered him,
then explained to Dan. "I lived up there a couple of
years ago with White Hair's band. They call him
Pahuska." He took a deep breath, his eyes far away. "I
left a squaw and some children up there."

Dan watched the Frenchman, and sensed something
coming that nobody could control. Even Poeyfarré, he
knew instinctively, would be powerless.

"You got to remember one thing," Simon said in his
ear. "These fellers are the best in the world at taking
care of themselves, but they are also children. They take

34

a notion to do something, they do it whether it's reasonable or not."

Dan looked at him. "You think he'll go back to the Osages?"

Simon shook his head. "Nobody knows . . . him least of all. Just keep your eyes skinned, for he left his squaw. If he goes back now, it means trouble. They'll know he's with our train, and they'll follow him to us." Simon frowned. "If he goes back to see his squaw, you can bet your life on one thing: the Indians won't stop him, because they know he'll lead them to us."

A cloud began to form in the west just before the sun went down. "We'll stop and make camp for a thunderstorm," said Poeyfarré. "There'll likely be some weather to-night."

Chamillard showed them how to arrange two pack-saddles close together, lay their rifles across them a foot above the ground, hang their bullet pouches and powderhorns on them, cover the whole with branches and lay a blanket over the branches, and finally with a scalping-knife dig a trench around the saddles and their burden. "If it rains, the water will run off," he said. "Dig a trench off to one side, and you can sleep inside. If it rains, you won't get too wet. *Oui?*"

"We'll dig," said Dan.

All the *voyageurs* were making the same preparations. The black cloud seemed to grow from within itself, and to expand more swiftly as it got bigger. Lightning flashes appeared in it, and occasionally a sonorous roll of thunder came to them as from a great distance.

The mules were loose-herded in a meadow below them, guarded by two men with rifles. "Your friends from the Six Bull River won't bother us to-night," said Poeyfarré to Chamillard, "but I look for them when it gets light."

Chamillard had a far-away look in his eyes. "Maybe they won't bother us," he said.

Poeyfarré snorted. "I don' like the look in your eye, you green-shelled turtle. You are getting ready for trouble."

There was a peal of thunder, closer than before, and Chamillard laughed the high, crazy laugh of a man who is drunk beyond control. "You never knew a squaw like Oak Leaf," he said in a detached voice.

Poeyfarré sounded disgusted. "I've known more squaws than you ever saw, *enfant*, and I found out one thing: a squaw is a squaw — Slave, Chippewa, Pottawatomie, Osage, or Wichita. If you don' get that damn' tone out of your voice, I am tempt' to hit you over the head."

Chamillard didn't even hear him. "You never had a squaw like Oak Leaf," he said as if from a vast fund of superior wisdom. "She makes you forget there are others of any tribe."

"Fool!" snarled Poeyfarré.

Menard came up. "It's on his own head," he said.

Poeyfarré looked about ready to battle. A yellow lightning flash illumined his projecting jaw, and his grey blue eyes were hard. "I don't care for his head. I care for mine. If he goes, he'll bring the Osages on us. That squaw he left before will report it the minute he steps out of her lodge."

"We'll be gone before the Osages get here."

"Not far enough," Poeyfarré insisted. "Who's watching the mules?"

"Villars and Brognard."

"You and I will relieve them."

Dan spoke up. "Simon and I will relieve you. We'll stand our turn."

Poeyfarré looked at him sceptically. "You know anything about Indians?"

"I been fighting Iroquois for ten years."

"They aren't like Osages."

"They work the same. Indians are pretty much Indians."

Poeyfarré nodded slowly. "One of you pair up with me, the other with Menard. We know this country, and you don't."

"All right."

Blackness now covered the entire sky. The air was heavy and oppressive, and lightning flashed in all directions but especially in the west. The interval between flashes had become so short that at times the sky presented a continuous succession of yellow forks which seemed to set off each other, and a minute afterward the valley below them was filled with the rolling thunder of the explosions. These came as sharp, titanic cracks more and more frequently. Then a cold wind struck them from the west. At first it merely shook the tree tops against the backdrop of lightning; then a few drops of rain came down.

Poeyfarré roared, "Get under cover! Stay away from trees! Menard, come with me!" and ran down the meadow towards the mule herd.

The wind howled through the trees, and Dan, inside his trench with the blanket around him, shuddered. The lightning now was almost a continuous sheet, and getting closer. The constant crash and roll of thunder made it impossible to talk. He sat there waiting for the storm to hit, and thought of Baltimore and Sarah Radnor.

He remembered the first thing he had noticed about Sarah, aside from her startling flaxen hair and violet eyes: she had a light, flowery fragrance, totally unlike his mother and sisters on the frontier, who invariably smelled of sour sweat and wood smoke. It had made him conscious of his buckskin clothes, but Sarah had insisted he wear them, even when she took him to society parties in Baltimore. She had exhibited him as she might have worn a large jewel or a rare miniature locket.

Sometimes it had annoyed him a little, but not too much. When he gazed down at her and saw the light in them that was for him only — for no woman could look that way at more than one man — then he didn't mind being introduced to her friends as a man of the frontier. Sometimes he had heard other words — "primitive," "straight from the jungle," "moves like a mountain cat" — but he did not let those disturb him, for Sarah's opinion only was important to him.

He thought of her now as he huddled in the blanket and waited for the storm to hit. Perhaps she was snugly asleep in her bedroom upstairs in Theophilus Radnor's big home; or at a party, drinking wine, perhaps tripping in the minuets at which he had been so clumsy — for, as she had said, his six-feet-three made him just too big to dance with ordinary people.

Lightning hit a little higher on the ridge. The hillside was as light as day, and the big trees shook with never-ending thunder. The wind shifted back to the west and blew straight up the meadow, driving the rain in horizontal sheets that penetrated everything — blanket, buckskin, meat, and bone. In the yellow light, Dan saw four men in the meadow keeping the mules together. The animals had turned their rumps to the rain and were holding ground. If they drifted at all, they would drift into the wind — not like cows, which would drift with the wind. Poeyfarré apparently understood this, for he and his men stood far behind the mules with their backs to the rain.

Poeyfarré and Menard came back after the storm centre passed over. All were wet through. They built a fire and took off their clothes to dry. They hung soaked blankets over the boughs of a fallen oak. Dan and Simon took axes and cleared a way to their rifles.

Poeyfarré was grumbling. "Storm like this, a man gets no sleep." He crammed a big pipe full of tobacco. "Only good thing, it keeps Osages in, too. They don't like this kind of weather any more than we do." He looked up at Dan. "Your rifles dry?"

"Dry enough."

"I saw three-four deer down there under the willows. See if you can get one. We'll be up all night anyway, so we might as well be eating."

Dan got his powder flask and took out the smaller flask of priming powder. He poured some on to the pan, and walked cautiously across the meadow, approaching the willows from the uphill side.

In the lightning flashes he saw the head of a buck, watching towards the east. He lay down in the wet grass and drew a careful aim. At the next flash he squeezed the trigger. The buck took one long leap into the water, but did not get up. Two does hit the water with great splashes and kept going. Simon came running down from camp. They carried the deer between them, and set it down by the fire. Poeyfarré's knife was already out. "Through the heart," he grunted. "That rifle of yourn shoots dead centre."

"It should," said Dan. "It was made by a good workman."

"None of these damn' French riflemakers, I hope."

"English."

"A good rifle," Poeyfarré grunted. "Wouldn't mind having one like that myself."

Dan looked at him in the firelight. "They're hard to come by," he said quietly.

Poeyfarré didn't notice — he was busy hanging strips of deer-meat over the fire on green twigs — but Simon looked up sharply.

Suddenly Poeyfarré turned. "Chamillard! Dartigo!" he roared.

There was no answer.

"Menard!"

"*Oui.*"

"Do you know anything about those two idiots?"

"No," Menard said carefully. "I have not see' them."

Poeyfarré uttered a string of nasal-sounding French oaths. He called down to the mule-herd. "Poupelinière!"

"*Oui,*" came the answer against the background of rumbling thunder and the whistling wind in the tree tops.

"Is Chamillard down there — or Dartigo?"

"*Non.*"

Poeyfarré shook his big head in a fury. "They've gone up to the Six Bull to hunt squaws," he muttered, "and if Chamillard finds Oak Leaf, he is certain to bring White Hair's band down on us."

CHAPTER
FIVE

Long before daylight they finished the deer, and Poeyfarré gave the order to start packing. "We have got to move," he said. "Chamillard's relatives will be after us." He groaned. "Why shouldn't that damn' fool wait until we got to the Wichita village? Worst of it is, they took two good mules."

They drove the mules hard until noon. "You will have to let them rest," Menard told Poeyfarré.

Poeyfarré grumbled but called a halt.

Dan and Brognard kept watch from the top of the hill while the others cooked a small doe that Dan had knocked over with a club.

Simon and Menard came up to act as lookouts and let the other two eat.

"Are we going on right away?" asked Brognard, a man with a deep scar running from one eye.

"Soon as we eat," said Menard, loading a pipe with tobacco.

"The mules won't keep it up much longer. They've got to have feed."

"Poeyfarré says they can eat at night. He says we've got to keep moving."

Brognard glanced to the north. They had not seen the Arkansa River all day. "Is no use to run anyway. The Osages can travel twice as fast as we can — and they can trail us clear to Santa Fé."

They went far over the cut-off that day, and before the sun went down they reached the Canadian Fork. Poeyfarré took the mules down to water, then established a camp in the middle of a sloping prairie between the river and a hillside covered with blackjack.

"Why not in the trees?" asked Dan. "We'd have cover."

"One man might do it," Poeyfarré said; "but a big outfit like this would get murdered. No white man can beat an Indian in the woods, and with six men and forty mules . . ." He shook his head. "We'll camp in the open. Indians don't like gunpowder and lead. They won't charge an open place like a white man."

It was quiet that night — too quiet, Poeyfarré said. He was up most of the night, prowling the camp, going alone down to the river or up towards the blackjack. He got them out before the sky turned grey in the east. They didn't eat, but packed the mules and headed south-west straight up the middle of the strip of prairie. It was good sense, Dan saw, because it would be difficult for any Indians to ambush them on the prairie.

The sun had just come up when a faint cry came: "Poeyfarré!"

Dan located the sound across the river. Two men were riding mules on the opposite ridge above the blackjack. He guessed they were Chamillard and

Dartigo, and he was glad they were back, for Chamillard had been friendly to him.

Poeyfarré waved at them but kept the train moving. Chamillard and Dartigo turned their mules and disappeared in the blackjack. Then, without warning and without sound, the rest of the hillside came alive.

There were redskins everywhere; every warrior was over six feet tall, dressed in breechclout and moccasins, with a beaverskin bandeau around the head. They had tattoed V's on the chests; their faces were painted black. Their scalps were shaved to leave only a strip of hair from front to back. And they were not making a sound.

"Like Mohawks," said Dan, reaching grimly for his rifle.

"No shooting now!" warned Poeyfarré. "It won't help them — and we've got to keep our rifles loaded for an attack on the train."

Poeyfarré and Menard were leading the mules into a circle.

"Unpack!" he shouted. "Tie the mules to each other so the Indians can't stampede them!"

A few shots came from the blackjack thicket, almost as a burst, and Dan looked soberly at Simon. "They couldn't have fired but twice," he said.

Simon was watching with narrowed eyes. He shook his head. "There was too many of 'em."

The mules began to graze. The six men spread themselves to face in all directions, using the pack-saddles as rifle rests. "They'll come from uphill — the blackjack — most likely." said Poeyfarré, "but watch in all directions. And don't everybody shoot at once. Take turns, so there's always a rifle loaded."

They herded the mules into a shallow draw and waited. Nothing moved for a long time, while the sun grew hotter. Then high in the air, almost too far to be visible, black dots began to circle over the blackjack where Chamillard and Dartigo had been last seen.

Dan, watching downstream in the direction from which they had come, saw a cayute walk up from the river, its nose high to catch the scents on the wind. Then a flock of prairie chickens — twenty or more — got up from the edge of the blackjack with a curious chicken-like cackling and flew almost over their heads and across the river to the other side.

Dan scanned the blackjack and saw the white tails of a dozen antelope as the animals floated out of sight over the ridge, and he knew then it was coming. "Poeyfarré!"

The big man grunted, nodding his head. "It'll probably come from there, all right — but you and Jeffreys keep an eye to the river. These Osages are tricky."

The first shot came from Menard. A bronze body with a fox-fur roach fell at the edge of the blackjack into the open prairie. Menard pulled his rifle down from the pack-saddle and began to reload it, lying on the ground, just as a flight of arrows came at the breastworks formed by the goods.

Poeyfarré fired. Another flight of arrows came at them. Dan heard one thud into a mule with that hard zip that he had come to recognise in the east.

For a while there was silence. Then a shot sounded from the blackjack. The ball went over their heads with a crack, and Dan looked for a small cloud of black smoke. He saw a gleam of bronze skin, a beaver bandeau. He centred the sights of the bandeau and let it go. An Indian dropped out of the tree.

Poeyfarré said, "I'm sure goin' to have one of them rifles, Shankle."

"They shoot centre," said Dan, "if you hold them right."

Menard laughed. Dan was on his back, reloading his rifle. Menard said, "If we don't get out of here, you don't need *any* kind."

"There's no *if*," said Poeyfarré. "I like my own head."

"The buzzards have settle' down across the rivaire," Brognard noted. "I theenk that's all of Chamillard and Dartigo."

Presently Menard observed, "The sun she's get' pretty high."

Brognard scowled. His scarred eye gave him a ferocious appearance. "And hot," he said.

Simon said, "Give me that bladder and I'll go for water."

"There'll be Indians at the river," said Poeyfarré. "That's where they want to drive us."

The mules soon began to bray for water. Poeyfarré swore. "The damn' Indians'll know we're short of water!"

"How long will they keep it up?"

"Till dark, most likely — unless they get tired of waiting and try to rush us. Then, if we make it hot for 'em . . ."

"They're come!" screamed Menard.

Poeyfarré shouted, "Stay down . . . and shoot straight!"

Osages erupted out of the blackjack with hideous yells and exploded across the grass towards the fort. Poeyfarré lay where he was, sighting along his rifle. Menard fired, and a big brave slid forward on his face. Simon got one between the eyes. Dan waited. Menard dropped his rifle and pulled a pistol from his waistband and cocked it.

Arrows were everywhere, but the men stayed down, and the Osages, now on a broad front, wavered. Back in the blackjack two roached braves stayed, one at each side, and attempted to provide a covering fire for the attackers. But here and there an Osage dropped, and the Indians didn't like it. The line wavered as it reached the dead mule. Menard stopped a black-faced warrior who fell across the mule's neck. Then the line broke. The Osages raced for the blackjack.

Poeyfarré got up on one knee. His face was black with powder smoke. "They forgot to yell goin' back," he said, and looked around. "Anybody hurt?"

"You got a bad hand," Dan observed.

Poetyfarré swore. "The damn' redskins! Why can't they shoot a man some place important instead of the base of his thumb?"

The thumb was hanging by a shred of skin. Poeyfarré looked at it disgustedly. He laid it on the pack-saddle and pulled out his knife. He took one chop and tossed his thumb into the dirt. "It'll be sore for a month," he growled. "Anybody else got anything?"

"I got a little here," said Dan, and straightened out his leg. The feathered end of an arrow shaft was almost up to his thigh. He began to cut off the protruding end.

Menard said. "You better have a drink, frien'."

Poeyfarré said, "Git the demijohn!"

It was Brognard who planted his moccasin against the back of Dan's thigh and pulled the arrow on through. He looked at Dan and laughed. "You're white in the face, Eenglishman!"

"I was scared by a ghost," said Dan, suddenly choking. "Give me that jug!"

An hour later he felt better. They had bandaged it with beaver fur to stop the bleeding, and he lay at full length, constantly flexing the leg to keep it from stiffening. The sun was hotter and the mules were braying louder.

"There's been no action up there for quite a while," said Menard. "Do you theenk they have retreated?"

Dan watched for a while. "There's a live Indian behind the mule," he announced. He took his skinning-knife from its sheath and tested the edge. "I can get him," he said, "if you keep them down up there at the blackjack."

"*Bien*," agreed Poeyfarré. "But don't let that Osage get the jump on you. We need every rifle we have."

Dan was flat, crawling out between two pack-saddles. "Keep them down, up there," he repeated.

He got out into the open. The grass was about six inches high and only half-covered him, but he stayed flat and progressed slowly under the sun. There was no breeze now. He heard a sandpiper in the river bed below, and from somewhere in the blackjack came the sad call of a wood phoebe. That was reassuring for it indicated that, if there were any Osages still in the blackjack, they were keeping low. And yet it was something to wonder about, for it didn't sound reasonable that they would desert a wounded companion. The Indian behind the mule, of course, should have been dead, but Dan had seen two very small movements of the roach, as if the Indian had been trying to get an eye on them.

He was half-way to the mule when a rifle crashed behind him, and he flattened out. An arrow dropped into the ground so close that it threw dust into his eyes. A prolonged "ah-ah-ah" came from the blackjack and ended in a gurgle that sounded as if the Indian had eggs in his throat and could no longer force his voice through. Or maybe it was blood.

He heard guttural words of Osage come from the blackjack, and he realised they were directed to the warrior behind the mule. That Indian was now warned and would be ready. He crawled on.

The mule had begun to swell up under the sun in spite of being gutshot, and big blue and green flies had settled around its nose and mouth.

Dan did not risk looking back. He wanted to be facing forward if and when the Osage came out from behind the mule. He moved almost without sound. A shadow passed over the ground and he knew the buzzards were circling, waiting for the end.

He could almost touch the mule now. Another shot sounded from the fort. This time there was no arrow, but from up ahead came the sound of an animal, fatally wounded, flopping a loose arm or leg in its death struggles. Like the Eastern Indians, Dan supposed, the Osages were hard to kill.

He could not see over the mule, and he dared not raise his head. He began to gather his feet under him. Then a single shouted word came from the blackjack, and he leaped to his feet.

The wounded Indian leaped at the same time, and for an instant they faced each other across the body of the mule. The Indian was a gruesome sight. He had taken the shot along the side of his head. Apparently it had not penetrated his skull, but it had cut a furrow in his scalp, and this had bled profusedly, until his face and chest were caked with dried blood already turning black.

Without a sound the Indian jumped at him, swinging a brass tomahawk. He ducked, and the tomahawk missed him, but the Indian's body hit him. He had braced himself to receive that impact, but he had not taken into full account his injured leg. He tried to turn on it, but it crumpled under him and he went down.

The bloody Indian dropped on him, with tomahawk raised. Dan rolled to free his right arm. Dan blocked the Indian's arm with his left forearm, and drove his knife up to the shaft in the bloody chest. The Indian tried to swing the tomahawk but failed. The light in the eyes died. The body slumped against Dan, who eased it to the ground, and went down with it to avoid presenting a target to the blackjack. He lay on his stomach in the protection of the mule's carcass and worked his knife out of the Indian. Then he began to reverse himself to start back for the improvised fort.

A "Don't!" from Simon stopped him. There were still Indians in the blackjack, then. Simon charged across the open space and threw himself at full length beside him.

"You hurt?" he asked.

"No."

"Poeyfarré thinks they've left the blackjack now that their *compañero* is out of the fight. I brought your rifle. Feel like going to have a look?"

"Sure." Dan wiped his knife on the Indian's bandeau and put it back in his sheath. He took the rifle. "You go up the left; I'll take the right. We'll meet in the middle."

Simon nodded. He glanced at Dan's leg, and watched him get up. "She's pretty stiff," he suggested.

Dan said, "Never mind. She'll limber up."

They moved out in a wide circle like a pair of curved horns. Poeyfarré and his men were watching. They reached the blackjack without trouble, and began to move from one tree to another.

They met in the centre. "No redskins," said Simon.

Dan shook his head. The leg was beginning to give him difficulty, and he could hardly walk on it.

The Frenchmen got to their feet as the two men returned. Poeyfarré nodded approval and turned to the mules. "Get these birds down to the water. You two —

Shankle and Jeffreys — stay here and keep an eye on things. We'll water the mules and then pack and move on. Can you ride?" he asked Dan.

"Don't worry about me," Dan told him. "Get some water into those mules before they bray themselves hoarse."

Poeyfarré grinned. He seemed relieved. He vaulted over the pack-saddles, and they began to untie the mules and turn them loose. Each one ran for the river.

Poeyfarré came back leading four animals by the halters. He looked worried. "I theenk we better cross the river and go up the other side this evening and to-morrow," he said. "If the Osages try to ambush us, they'll wait on this side, for they know the trail."

"What happens to the goods of Chamillard and Dartigo?" asked Villiers.

"We divide the goods and mules between us. They don't need them any more."

Within another hour the sun was nearing the western horizon. They took the trail down to the river. The water wasn't over a foot deep, but it was loaded with red silt. Dan rode a mule across and then dismounted and went upstream a way to drink. They crossed the half-mile bed of the river — most of it dry sand — and turned left on the sloping hillside where they had seen Chamillard and Dartigo.

Menard looked up to the blackjack. His face was drawn. "We ought to look for them," he said.

Dan was behind him. "I'll go with you. They might be alive."

52

The sun was half-way down now, and inside the blackjack thicket it was twilight. They rode through carefully, watching the ground. Menard swore under his breath and galloped the mule forward. A dozen vultures flapped heavily into the air in all directions, while Menard jumped off the mule, grabbed a fallen branch, and struck at the big birds, but they all were out of reach before he could hit them. He came back, swearing.

"There's no need to bury them, anyway."

"There's not much left to bury," said Dan.

They started after the train. "What I don't understand," said Dan, "is what happened to their heads. There weren't even any skull bones left."

"The Wazhazhe," said Menard.

Dan stared at him. "They cut them off?"

"That's the way they count coup — especially when they're mad."

Poeyfarré met them as they rode up. "What do you see?"

Menard shook his head. For a moment he could not talk.

Dan moved in the saddle to take his weight off his bad leg. "It looks like Chamillard and Dartigo found what they went after," he said; "but the price was pretty high."

CHAPTER
SIX

They camped on the ridge that night, out in the open. The next morning again they were up early, pushing towards the south-west. The following morning, Poeyfarré led them back across the Canadian Fork and they took up the former trail for several days. Then they broke away from the river and went almost due south around an area of low mountains.

Some days later they came to the shore of a much wider river, and camped near it in the early afternoon.

"This is the Red Rivaire of Natchitoches," Poeyfarré told them. "We'll cross here in the morning, and by night we'll be with the Pani Piqués."

"Why don't we cross to-night?"

"There may be trouble. She's a big rivaire and as tricky sometimes as the Osages."

"I don't theenk we have trouble this time," said Menard.

Poeyfarré studied it. "Maybe not so. There is not so much water as last time. We'll have to swim the mules, though."

He had them build their fire in a draw and burn the bone-dry cottonwood before dark, so the light would not be reflected from the trees or rocks. "We are only a little way from Spanish territory," he said, "and I do not want to wake up in the morning and find a troop of Spanish dragoons waiting for us on the other side. It's better to get to the villages first and get our trading done. Then there is no trouble."

They swam the mules across the next morning before the sun was up. Poeyfarré led out, feeling his way across, swimming his mule in the deepest part. The pack mules, kept in place by the six men, followed quietly. One or two objected to swimming but were pulled into the stream by rawhide ropes around the necks, and had no choice. They gathered on the south shore and strung out along the river. By sunrise they had gone quite a distance, and Poeyfarré was satisfied. The country was mostly undulating prairie, and they marked down several small buffalo herds, but Poeyfarré would not let them hunt.

Menard, who had now attached himself to Dan and Simon, said, "He's always nervous when he gets near."

"Scared of the Spanish?" asked Simon.

"Eet ees not alone the Spanish. One does not know how friendly the Panis may be."

About noon the train reached a smaller stream that flowed into the Red River, and Poeyfarré led them up the south bank. The stream was twenty feet wide by one foot deep, but its water was clear and sweet, and for the first time in several days the mules were allowed to drink all they wanted.

"They've seen us," said Poeyfarré.

"How do you know?" asked Simon.

Poeyfarré pointed to the south-west. "See that column of smoke? They make it by throwing green leaves on a fire. That notifies the chief there's company coming."

"You're scary," said Simon.

Poeyfarré swept off his red stocking cap and bent his head towards them. "You see that? That hair has been there all my life."

Menard laughed, but Poeyfarré went on seriously, "Is one thing I am ver' finical about: I don' want to lose my scalp."

Two hours later they were riding into a large flat space surrounded by low hills and opening on the river — a sort of amphitheatre on the prairie. To Dan's surprise they rode through fields of corn, pumpkins, melons, squashes, and beans. A mile away across the fields were about two hundred peculiar straw structures, round, and tapering to a point at the top.

Among the straw dwellings were numerous upright racks made of boughs, upon which were hung thousands of dark objects that Menard said were thin slices of buffalo meat for drying. But Menard didn't like the look of things. "The kids are all inside," he said. "Even the squaws are under cover."

"Maybe," said Brognard, "they don' know who we are yet."

"It is something to hope," Poeyfarré growled. "Whatever happens, don't fire a rifle or draw a knife unless I say so."

Chills began to play up and down Dan's spine. The village seemed deserted, but meat was still on the drying racks . . . Then suddenly the village erupted Indians, who poured towards them afoot and on horseback, with fearful yells.

"Keep going," ordered Poeyfarré. "No faster, no slower."

Menard observed, "I don' theenk they on the warpath. Squaws and kids come, too. Anyhow, when they fight they hide. They no attack like this."

It seemed that Menard was right. It was frightening to be surrounded by hundreds of Indians whose skins were so dark that they were almost black, but they offered no harm. They were shorter than the Osages, and heavier. Their faces were broad, their noses were flat, and their hair was long and black, neither combed nor braided.

The men wore moccasins, leggings, and breach-clouts or flaps; the women wore moccasins and short bark skirts, with nothing above the waist; their faces were heavily tattoed, and intricate rings were tattooed around their breasts. The men were not tattooed at all.

Poeyfarré kept the train moving, his rifle balanced across his saddle. A smaller party came from within the village of grass huts. These, too, were all on foot but one, who rode a barebacked mule. This Indian was huge and grossly fat. He wore the usual moccasins and leggings, a breech-clout, and a blue silk shirt. He pulled up to Poeyfarré, who grinned and said, "*Hartch.*"

"*Hartch!*" the fat Indian said.

Poeyfarré balanced the rifle with his knees while he clasped his hands before him. "We come in peace," he said.

The fat chief nodded. He held his right hand, back up, before his left breast, and moved it briskly to the front.

Menard sighed gratefully. "He says we're welcome."

"Is that the Indian sign language?" asked Dan.

"Sure," said Simon. "You don't see it in the east. This is about as far as it comes."

"We bring plenty *wayco*, plenty *eteh-cod*, plenty of tobacco and gunpowder," said Poeyfarré.

The big chief smiled widely. "It is a long time since the Natchitoches traders have brought us anything worth having. Beads and looking-glasses — they are fine for women, but a warrior needs other things."

They palavered for a while, sometimes in sign language, sometimes in Wichita, sometimes in Spanish, and with a few French words thrown in, and finally Poeyfarré nodded, satisfied. He turned to them, and all the tenseness was gone from his face. "It's all right. Chief Eyasiquiche says we can camp just beyond the village, and to-morrow we'll do some trading. The village across the river will come over, too." He rubbed his hands briskly. "It looks good. There haven't been any other traders here since last year."

"Can't we start trading?" asked Simon.

"To-morrow. Any hurry?"

"I just like to get it settled."

"If you start swapping too soon, you won't get much. Let these Panis celebrate to-night. Pour a little whisky in 'em, and to-morrow they'll be twice as easy to deal with."

By this time it was dark, and a big fire was built in the centre of the village. Dan and Simon and Menard were led to a conical grass-thatched hut. Poeyfarré and Brognard and the taciturn Poupelinière were given a hut opposite them, and all unloaded their goods around the dwellings. "You can turn the mules loose," said Poeyfarré. "They will go to the river for water, and the Wichitas will take care of them to-night."

They went up to the fire, and Eyasiquiche, resplendent in his blue silk shirt, sat cross-legged on the ground, his vast bulk having long ago popped off the buttons until now it was open at the front at least a foot when he sat down.

The braves gathered around the fire, and all ate buffalo out of a big brass kettle, fishing out pieces with their knives, biting into them, sometimes throwing them back into the pot if they didn't like the piece.

Finally they passed around a pipe, each Indian and all the members of the trading party taking a whiff until it had been around several times. Then Poeyfarré produced a demijohn. Eyasiquiche's eyes lighted up. He turned up the jug and took a huge drink.

Dan observed, "At that rate it'll be gone before it gets to us."

Brognard's good eye was gleaming. "Don' worry, my frien'. Poeyfarré is no fool. He has plenty of those."

Dan felt mellow when they went back to the huts, but he hardly sat down on the straw pallet when an Indian came in the open door, unannounced. "*Kah-haak!*" he said grandly.

Menard looked up. In the semi-darkness, lighted by the fire from the centre of the village, Menard's eyes glittered. "*Atch-kinch?*"

The Wichita shrugged. "*Cha-osth, witch, taw-way . . .*"

"What's he talking about?" asked Dan.

"I got a notion," said Simon, swallowing.

The Wichita turned to him. His left hand was out, fingers together, thumb extended. He closed his right hand into a fist, with the index finger extended, and brought the two hands together, index finger lying between the thumb and other fingers of the left hand.

Dan sat back. "Not for me, I guess."

"You're gonna be lonesome," said Menard.

The Wichita stepped aside, and three Wichita girls came in. None was over sixteen; their bodies were husky and firm, their breasts full and solid. Menard said, "I'll take two!"

Simon held out a hand, and said, "One of these is enough for me."

Menard had a girl on each side of him, and was talking in low tones, when the Wichita came back and fired a string of Indian words at him.

Menard got up on one elbow. "Eyasiquiche wants to know if you weren't satisfied, Shankle."

Dan looked up. "It isn't that."

"He says you can have your pick of the whole village."

Dan said, "Tell him, thanks. The women look very good, but tell him I have a wife at home. Tell him the white man takes only one wife."

"They'll think there's something wrong with you."

Dan said finally, "Maybe there is."

He woke up about daylight. Menard's girls were just leaving, and Simon said, "I didn't know you was married, Dan."

"I'm not," Dan said, "but I . . ."

"Baltimore is a long way from here."

"I know — but I expect *her* to remember *me*."

"Anybody I know?" asked Simon.

Dan pulled on his hunting-shirt. "Sarah Radnor."

"Daughter of old Theophilus?"

"Yes."

One of the Wichita girls appeared suddenly, without sound, flashed a big smile, and set a small kettle of savoury meat in the centre of the hut.

Simon fished a piece of meat out of the kettle. "Never thought you'd marry a girl like Sarah."

Dan frowned and stared at Simon.

"For one thing," said Simon, stripping a hump rib between his teeth, "she's a society woman; she couldn't live on the frontier."

"Somebody has to live in the cities," said Dan, reaching with his knife.

"And for another thing, she isn't interested in *any* man."

"What do you mean by that?"

"But NO offence," said Simon stubbornly. "You can forget this when you get back, and I reckon you better, but all any man will ever be to Sarah Radnor is something to show off, like a piece of jewellery — something that will draw attention to her."

CHAPTER
SEVEN

Dan went outside. The air was fresh and clean. Only a few persons were moving this morning, and they were squaws, tending the fire and cooking big kettles of buffalo meat. The three men went down to the stream, and Dan was scratching. Menard looked at him and grinned. "Lice, eh?"

"Don't let it worry you," said Simon. "You can get 'em off by scrubbing with sand."

"What about clothes? Burn them?"

"Come weeth me," said Menard. "I show you a very good way."

They walked across the prairie until they found a big ant hill. "Take off your clothes," said Menard, "and pile them up on top of the hill. When you get back, you will have only ants to get rid of."

"And you do that by shaking them," said Simon.

Dan began to take off his shirt. "I'm going to look funny as hell running around over the prairie naked."

"Don't worry," Menard advised. "These *Indians* are not afflicted with modesty. It would surprise them if you refused to take off your clothes."

They walked back naked to the stream. The water was clear and sweet, and Dan had one of the most enjoyable baths he had taken in a long time.

A Wichita girl came to the stream with two buffalo paunches for water. She watched them in the stream, and smiled.

"Only one thing about it," Dan said on the way back to the ant hill. "I've got too much Connecticut blood in me, I guess. I'd feel better if the water was more than a foot deep."

They found their clothes thoroughly de-loused. The ants had done a good job. They whipped out the ants and put on the clothes.

"Now you're all set until to-night," Simon observed.

"To-night," said Dan, stepping around a prickly pear cactus, "I'm sleeping in the middle of the floor."

They entered the village. "What do we do now?" asked Simon. "When do we start making a few piastres?"

"Sometime this afternoon Eyasiquiche will be ready — and don't trade cheap. A rifle is worth from ten to twenty mules out here."

"I didn't bring rifles."

"Poeyfarré did. They're hidden now for fear of the Spanish, but they are here and Eyasiquiche knows it, or he wouldn't be so friendly."

They got back to the hut, and Dan built a fire with flint and steel and put on some coffee. "What about the glass beads and vermilion, and mirrors and sugar? Is that all wasted?"

Menard was lying on his side with his head propped on one hand. "Sure, that is standard trade goods, and they'll take it, but if we didn't have rifles, powder, lead, and flints, they'd let us camp out on the prairie and watch our own mules. I've seen a rifle buy four young squaws from the Camanches." He looked curiously at Dan. "You never did any Indian trading down here, did you?"

"No."

"Why then did you risk your hair coming this way?"

Dan looked up. He saw Menard's eyes, speculating. He pushed a couple of sticks under the coffee bucket. "There was no guarantee I could get a trading licence in Natchitoches," he said shortly.

The village was beginning to awaken. Poeyfarré came from the chief's tent, looking better than he had since the trip started. "The redskins'll be ready to start trading as soon as they get their bellies full and have a couple of pipes," he said. "And good news, Menard. It's been a dry summer, and Toroblanco's band of Camanches are only a couple of days away."

Simon asked quickly, "What does that figure up to?"

"After a dry summer, the Camanches will be impatient to trade. The Wichitas will have a quick turnover, so they can afford to make some good deals."

The Wichitas ate about mid-forenoon, and took their time. Poeyfarré was pow-wowing with Eyasiquiche, and many pipes were passed around. Poeyfarré got two jugs of whisky to follow the pipes. The Wichita women were standing beyond the circle of men. "You can unwrap your beads pretty soon now," Menard told Dan.

But there was a rising murmur of voices through the village, and movement. Menard stood up. "Damn!" he said. "There's another pack train coming."

"From the Arkansa?" asked Dan.

Menard shook his head. "It must be from Natchitoches."

"Maybe Spanish officials."

"Maybe, but they won't dare do anything to us out here. The Indians are too strong." He watched. "I don't see any soldiers. It's likely a trader."

Simon swore. "That'll drive prices down."

The pack train approached the village. There were a dozen mules and three muleteers. The village went to meet them, while Poeyfarré sat by the fire. "A mighty lot of good whisky I wasted," he said glumly.

Dan watched. Some of the packs were made up of long, narrow, wooden boxes.

Eyasiquiche, with the help of two braves, was mounting his mule and going to meet the train.

Dan straightened. He stared at a black-bearded man who stopped to powwow with Eyasiquiche. Pretty soon the train started on through the village. Dan took a few steps forward.

The black-bearded man looked at him without particular interest at first. Then his eyes widened and he scowled a little. He glanced at Dan's length and then back at his face.

Dan took a step forward. "John Meservy," he said. "Last time I saw you was in Baltimore."

Meservy seemed to make his answer cautiously, probingly. "Last time I saw you, you were in Baltimore yourself."

"Things change," said Dan.

Meservy seemed to be studying him, trying to penetrate his thoughts. "It's queer we should end up at the same Indian village . . . so far away."

"It's queer," said Dan, "but perhaps not unexpected."

Hardness came into Meservy's dark eyes. He turned his back on Dan. "Keep 'em going in the rear there!" he shouted.

Meservy's train moved past, and Dan returned to the circle that now included only Simon and some Frenchmen.

"Friend of yours?" Simon asked.

"Hard to tell. He came to Baltimore after you left. Supposed to be a broker."

Simon eyed him shrewdly. "Was it him you came out here to find?"

"I wasn't exactly surprised to see him," Dan admitted.

"You looked it."

Dan studied the hills across the village. "It was a thing I had thought of, but not a thing I really expected."

Simon worked off a chew. "He's sure going to ruin our business with the Wichitas. No doubt you noticed," he said dryly, "that half of them mules carried rifles."

"It probably won't hurt our business as much as it will Poeyfarré's. We'll still have looking-glasses and stuff."

66

"Maybe this Meservy has, too."

Dan didn't answer.

"One thing is sure," said Simon. "We've got him in our backyard and I've got a feeling we'll have dealings with him. Maybe you better tell me something about him."

Dan watched Meservy turn into an open place near a haystack curiously set up on a framework and boughs so that it was several feet above the ground, and equally protected by a dirt-and-straw-covered roof like the one on their own beehive dwelling. "Maybe I'd better," he said heavily.

Simon said, with some sarcasm in his voice, "It's nice to learn this is more than just a business deal between you and me."

"I didn't want to draw you into it. I thought, with me putting up the money and you going along to furnish experience and help, it was a fair enough deal."

"The deal was all right, but what about Meservy? What if he decides to eliminate both of us from competition?"

"Remember when you and I got back from sailing around the world on the *Caroline*?" said Dan.

"Pretty well. We anchored to a post off the levee, and everybody went into New Orleans to celebrate. You got in a hell of a fight with the bosun over a Creole girl in a saloon. That was just after the Spanish took over Louisiana — 1766, wasn't it?"

"Yes."

"You laid the bosun over the bar and might' near broke his neck. Then you disappeared with the Creole girl and two others, and turned up four days later looking like a dish rag. You was a pretty good man in those days," he noted; "but now you act like you was ninety years old."

"I can still see an attractive woman as far as you can shoot a rifle and then some," Dan said spiritedly. "Only thing is, I got a little mixed up in Baltimore and I'm trying to figure my way out."

"One of them Wichita squaws could help considerable."

"It might be, but I have to see my way clear first."

"Out here," Simon suggested, "you're as good as a million miles away. These Wichita girls don't expect you to marry 'em."

"I know that, but what if I decided I'd rather have one of them, and wanted to stay here on the Red River?"

Simon raised his eyes. "You could do a lot worse. A good man, married into the Wichitas, could make a fortune for himself and his friends. You could control all the trade that comes through here. Don't forget: this is the trading centre of all northern Rejas."

"That still doesn't take Sarah Radnor's feelings into account."

Simon just stared at him, but his thoughts were plain in his calculating eyes. Why worry about Sarah Radnor? She'd do all the worrying necessary about herself.

Dan frowned. It made him most uncomfortable. Simon was right: Sarah spent most of her time looking out for herself — now that he was fifteen hundred miles away in savage country and could see it clearly. But nevertheless she had a strong hold on him even at that distance. It annoyed him, but he couldn't see what to do about it. After all, he *had* asked her. He got up and went to the fire under the coffee pot. He got a coal, lit his cigar, and puffed it into a red glow at the tip.

"When we came back on the *Caroline*," he said, "I shipped out to Baltimore, and when I got home I found my father had been killed in the French and Indian War while I was gone. My mother had been given some land scrip, and she wanted me to go to the Wyoming Valley in eastern Pennsylvania. It was a nice valley and fertile soil, and we held our own. The land had cost Mother nothing, and we made good crops, which we generally took to Philadelphia or Baltimore for trade."

Two Wichita girls, full-bodied and full-breasted, passed them carrying empty buffalo paunches. They looked at the two men and smiled. Simon grinned broadly, and Dan nodded.

"Meantime," Dan went on, "John Meservy came to Baltimore and set up as a broker. He claimed to be a Yankee from Connecticut, but nobody ever believed him. He didn't talk like a Yankee. He talked like a Britisher. However, he had plenty of money, and so the talk died down."

"This happened while you were in Wyoming Valley?"

"Yes."

He watched Meservy stop the two Wichita girls and talk to them. To Dan's astonishment, Meservy seemed to be using the Wichita language. "Nobody ever was sure how he made his money," said Dan. "He didn't do much brokerage business, but he blossomed out with a fine carriage and fancy clothes and a team of blooded horses. I remember when he first drove down along the docks. I had brought in a wagonload of furs and was buying sugar and cocoa, needles and pins, nails and raw wool to take back home, and Meservy was quite a grand man in his pigtail wig with a red satin ribbon, a three-cornered hat trimmed in ostrich feather, and blue silk stockings with golden clocks."

Simon spat at the ground.

"And you didn't know where he came from?"

"He arrived on the stage from Philadelphia, but how he got to Philadelphia was always a subject of speculation."

"What did he have to do with you aside from the fact that you disliked him?"

"Did I say I disliked him?"

"It's obvious."

Dan sighed. "My next younger sister Georgina — the one you were fond of — had married a clerk of Theophilus Radnor, and had two children. She was very attractive, as you may recall."

"She was so beautiful and so gracious that I quit saving myself when I heard she was married, and decided to go to hell the quickest way."

Dan sighed. "Georgina married for love, and her husband was a good catch. He was presentable, knew his way around Baltimore, was well thought of, worked hard, and would have owned his own business sooner or later. Besides, he could see no woman but Georgina."

"It sounds as if they were a match."

70

"They were. Then Meservy hired him to make a trip to the West Indies for rum."

"And he was lost overboard?"

"You're a suspicious man. Anyway, it looked to be a good trip for Georgina's husband, for he was on a commission, and when he returned he should have been able to set up his own brokerage. At that time, too, Meservy had never exchanged words with Georgina except on public occasions, so nothing was thought of it. But fate played into his hands. The ship ran into the great West Indian hurricane of 1772, and Georgina's husband was lost overboard." Dan scowled. "Then Meservy began paying suit to Georgina. He was a clever scoundrel, and it all seemed straight and above-board."

"How did you find out it wasn't?"

"Georgina rejected him flatly. She told me later that he had made improper advances before the news came that her husband was lost."

"Georgina always was a girl with spirit."

"She still is." Dan glanced at Simon. "Mother and I and my younger sister Maria were on the farm, and I was the only man, with Georgina's husband gone." He paused. "Some people didn't think Georgina would fit in, being used to fine clothes and parties, but they were wrong. She wore coarse dresses and worked like a farmhand, as any woman has to do on the frontier. She didn't scare a bit when the Indians came in, either."

"Maybe," said Simon, "I ought to go back."

"Then," said Dan, "we got mixed up in a war between the Pennsylvanians and the Connecticut

Yankees, and all the time there were Indians — Cayugas, Senecas, Delawares, Shawnees, and strays. For me it was mostly fighting while the women did the farm work. They tilled the fields and took care of the stock, but it was a right nice piece of land and the women did well."

"And Georgina — ?"

"Georgina minded her own business. Several nice young fellows courted her, but she stayed at work and raised her kids. She said as long as she could do for herself she didn't want some other man to take care of her kids. Anyway, I guess she had been pretty much in love with her husband."

"But something's all wrong," said Simon shrewdly. "There's no man on your place at all, and now you're down here, so you certainly didn't come down here just to trade with the Indians."

"No. No, I guess not." Dan smoked for a moment. "A while back our wagons began to return empty from Baltimore. We sent flour and whisky and hogmeat down, and got nothing back but money."

"What's wrong with money?"

"No objection to money — either pounds or piastres — but it's no good of itself. It's worthless if you can't use it to buy goods — clothing, ploughshares, cloth, needles, axes, and rifles. The Indians were getting rifles from the French and British, and they were better armed than we were. The only gunpowder we could get came in driblets from Philadelphia, and finally one man in the valley set up a powder mill, but saltpetre was hard to come by, and his powder wasn't very good,

72

anyway. So I went down to Baltimore to ask Theophilus Radnor why our money wasn't any good. Theophilus was indisposed that day, and they sent me to his home." Dan took a deep breath. "That was when I first met Sarah face to face."

CHAPTER
EIGHT

He had ridden up the sand-covered driveway of the Radnor grounds, knowing he was out of place but not knowing how to avoid it. He tied his horse's reins to one of the iron weights near the front door, went up, and used the brass knocker. A black woman in a white uniform and little white cap came to the door.

"Deliv'ries at the b . . ." she said, but then she took in the length of him and the breadth of his shoulders, his coon-skin cap and long-fringed hunting-shirt; her eyes went to his horse and back to him, and when they returned they were considerably bigger. "Did you wish to see somebody, suh?"

"Mr. Radnor . . . if he's able to see anyone."

"Yas, suh." She hesitated, and again he felt ill at ease. He wasn't used to such fancy doings; on the frontier you either walked in or started ducking bullets. "Mebbe you better come in, suh," she said at last.

There was elegance even in the maid's appearance, he realised, as his eyes became adjusted to the dimness and he surveyed the room in which he was now alone. *Elegant* was the only word to describe it — altogether by far the fanciest place he had ever seen. What good it was he didn't rightly know; it made a man think of a king's castle as he imagined it must be, but it was astonishing to find such a thing right here in Baltimore.

He was still standing in the centre of the room, surveying its ornate furnishings, when a clear voice asked, "You wish to see my father?"

It took him a while to locate her, for she was only minute-size. She was standing in an ivory-framed doorway that he hadn't noticed, and he was vaguely aware that she was standing there purposely, for the duskiness of the ivory was a complement to her clear skin and brought out the gleaming highlights in her flaxen hair.

"I . . . yes, ma'am, I came to speak with him."

She moved a few steps closer, almost floating. "At the moment he is rather ill. Won't you sit down?"

Though conscious of his dirty leggings and hunting-shirt, he decided he had better sit down, and he did, taking care to sit straight and not lean against the back, and to keep his feet on the floor so that his leggings would not rub against the chair.

She sat opposite him, and there was no hint in her voice or manner that he didn't belong there. It gave him a special feeling of attachment to her from the start.

"You're Dan Shankle, aren't you?"

"Yes, ma'am."

"You could hardly be anyone else," she murmured. "Won't you take off your cap? You may find it cooler."

He swept off the coon-skin and held it on one knee.

"You're from Wyoming Valley, aren't you?"

"Yes, ma'am."

"We in Baltimore have heard of your exploits on the frontier, Dan. Won't you tell me about them?"

"There's nothing much to tell, ma'am. We just went up there to make a farm, and the Senecas and Cayugas didn't want us there. They tried to run us off and we fought back, ma'am. That's all."

But her violet eyes were glowing in their depths. "How about the time you fought five of them, single-handed, with a knife, and killed all of them? It's all over New England how you vanquished the entire party?"

"Yes, ma'am, but they invited it. We weren't looking for trouble. They waited at the spring and captured our next-door neighbour about sun-up as she went for water."

"And you?"

"Her youngest boy came after me, because the oldest boy was taking a boatload of skins down to Louisburgh on the Susquehanna. I took my rifle and pistol and went after them."

"And your knife?"

"Yes, ma'am, we always carry a knife and a tomahawk."

"Into the woods alone after five savage Indians!" she exclaimed.

"Well, you see, they were burdened with having to handle Mrs. Cotlow as well."

"And Mrs. Cotlow . . . Was she pretty?"

"A woman any man would be proud to have on the frontier, ma'am, but not like you. That is to say, it's hard work living on the frontier, raising half a dozen children, cutting wood, ploughing, fighting Indians. A lady has little time to spend on fixing-up."

"And yet you say she was pretty?"

"Yes, ma'am, one of the prettiest women I ever saw . . . except in Baltimore."

"And you caught up with them?"

"Well, ma'am, Mrs. Cotlow is not a woman who likes to be manhandled; she was putting up a battle, and I trailed them and caught up to them as they were trying to get her across the river in a canoe."

"And you attacked them?"

"Well, ma'am, I didn't dare shoot at the Indians, for they were struggling with her and I might have hit her, so I put a bullet through the boat below the waterline."

"I thought women usually killed themselves when they were captured by Indians."

"No, ma'am, not often. First place, it isn't always easy; second place, they often escape."

"But Indians!" she said with a fine distaste in the thinning of her lips. "They smell, don't they?"

"Yes, ma'am. As for that, I guess we all smell after we've been out there a while."

"Tell me about the fight."

He had got over his self-consciousness now, and began to feel easier. "Not much to tell. I ran up to them and began laying into them with my tomahawk."

"I thought it was a knife."

"Not at first, ma'am. I finished the last one off with a knife, and used it to raise their hair after it was all over, but the main fighting was done with the tomahawk."

"Is that it that you have on your left side now?"

"Yes, ma'am, I . . ."

"Do you mind if I see it?"

"Why, no, ma'am, I . . . it isn't much to see . . . just a sort of brass hatchet with a sharp edge." He drew it from the rawhide loop and handed it to her, handle first. "It's heavy, as you can see, and makes a good weapon when there's room to swing it."

He expected her to touch the hatchet gingerly, but she took the handle in her small white hand and hefted the hatchet to get its balance, and he at once admired her for it.

"You killed four Indians with this tomahawk?"

"Yes, ma'am, in a manner of speaking."

"That is, you . . ."

She looked up, bright-eyed, obviously fascinated by the picture of him swinging the tomahawk. "Where do you . . . hit them with it?"

"We generally aim for the top of the head somewhere . . . try to get through the skull."

She shuddered exquisitely. "And you scalped them?" she asked finally.

"Well . . . yes, ma'am. They scalp us if they can," he said defensively.

"What do you do with the . . . scalps?"

He put the tomahawk back in its loop. "Hang them up in the sun somewhere — far enough away so they don't stink up the house."

"We hear so much about Indian fighting, but I've never seen a scalp."

"I'd be glad to send you one, one, ma'am, next time I get a chance."

78

She arose. "I'd better see about father. If you will wait . . ."

She was gone before he realised it. Like most small women, she moved fast. He watched the doorway where she had disappeared.

He now felt at ease. In spite of his buckskin clothing, his coon-skin cap, and his moccasins, Sarah Radnor had made him feel at home. He looked down at his clothes and was grateful that he had thought to take a bath in the creek the day before he reached Baltimore.

He studied the magnificence of the room he was in, and then heard the silken rustle of Sarah's dress. She seemed to materialise in the doorway.

"Father doesn't feel like talking to-day, but he suggests that you stay with us a few days until he feels better."

"But, ma'am, I can't . . ."

She moved closer. "Of course you can," she said with a smile. "The Indians can wait."

"I don't think . . ."

"Have you got a wife?"

"No, ma'am, just my mother and two sisters, but —"

"I'm sure they wouldn't begrudge you a rest."

He was suddenly reluctant to leave her. "Maybe."

"All Baltimore is talking about your exploits. Surely you can stay a fortnight and let them have a look at a real frontiersman."

"Not a fortnight, ma'am. I couldn't stay away that long."

"Then two or three days," she coaxed.

"All right." He justified himself on the ground that he did have to see Theophilus Radnor.

"The maid will show you to your room. We'll have supper in about an hour."

He got up. She came closer to him and took his big hand in her two small ones. Her hands were unexpectedly warm. "I'm glad you're going to stay," she whispered.

The closeness of her, the fragrance of the lavender, the intimate friendliness in the depths of her eyes, the warmth and pressure of her hands — all these things were like a draught of rye whisky on an empty stomach. They had him reeling for a moment, and then he swallowed, and said, "I'd better see about my horse."

"The groom will put your horse in the stable."

"But, miss, these are the only clothes I have."

She smiled. "I wouldn't for the world have you wear anything else. It would destroy the entire effect."

He didn't quite know what she meant, but he followed the maid to the bedroom. This was a large room but not as richly furnished as the parlour. A round braided rug occupied the centre of the open floor. A dresser stood at one wall, with a heavy china pitcher and washbasin. The bed, however, took up about half of the room. It was a huge affair, with a post at each corner that extended almost to the ceiling, and from a framework around the top hung a silk canopy. A decorated bootjack stood alongside the bed, and a round brass bed-warmer with a long handle was against the wall.

80

Dan took one look at all this splendour, and was dubious about sleeping the first night, but he would certainly try. He put his rifle in a corner, hung his power horn and bullet bag on pegs, tossed his coon-skin cap on the floor under the bed. There was water in the pitcher, and he washed his face and hands, and was a little astonished at the amount of dirt on them. He dried on a linen towel that seemed far too fine for such ordinary use, and remembered to take the half-used carrot of tobacco from the wallet formed by his wrap-around leather shirt and drop it into his coon-skin cap under the bed.

The window was genuine glass, and he could look out at the stable, with half a dozen stalls, and two blacks currying fine horses. They'd have a time currying his, he thought. That horse never had seen a curry comb; all it wanted was a good roll in the dirt.

He had dinner that night, and used the knife and fork the best he could ; he didn't see they were much improvement over a scalping knife. He realised that he'd have to get rid of the tomahawk until he was ready to go back. The thing would be scratching up the furniture.

Sarah sat opposite him at the table, and he had never seen such a beautiful girl. "Father is still not very well," she said, "though he is improving, and I think will be able to see you to-morrow. But to-night I am taking you to a reception at Lord Thaxted's."

He gulped. "I can't go to a place like that. I'm not properly dressed."

A gleam of intensity was in her eyes. "You must believe me, Dan; you will take Baltimore by storm. They have never seen such a man as you."

Nevertheless, he felt uncomfortable about it. Later he found that even the carriage wasn't made for a man of his height.

Lord and Lady Thaxted soon put him at ease, and Sarah took him everywhere and introduced him to so many persons that he could not begin to keep them separated in his mind. They had punch made of brandy and rum, which he discovered was quite as potent as rye whisky or plain peach brandy. They danced the minuet and the Virginia reel to the tune of two fiddles and a bass viol, and the ladies, after they had once stared at him, seemed to forget that he was dressed differently, and instead gathered around him while Sarah encouraged him to tell of the five Cayugas he had chased to the river bank. His audience seemed to grow until there were few left to dance.

It was then that John Meservy appeared. He was a tall man, but still three or four inches less than Dan. His dress, however, was quite different. He wore a heavily powdered wig, an apple-green coat with a white ribbed silk waistcoat and a frill of linen filling the V; his black silk breeches were very tight and ended at the knees; his long stockings were white silk with gold clocks, and his leather shoes had square toes, large silver buckles, and red heels. In all this magnificence he looked at Dan, tucked his ivory cane under one arm, took a tiny golden snuff-box from his waistcoat, dropped a pinch of snuff on the back of one hand, and sniffed it into his long Roman nose.

Dan, suddenly, feeling foolish, had stopped his tale. Meservy took his time, getting all eyes on him, and then looked up. "It is quite obvious," he said, pointedly staring at Dan's clothes, "that this gentleman is at home chasing Indians through the forest."

Dan hardened and spoke before he thought. All the bitterness of his knowledge of Meservy came out in one harsh sentence. "I send no woman's husband to sea to make her a widow."

He heard gasps around him, and instantly regretted having spoken. But then he realised that Meservy might challenge him to a duel, and he felt better. He would welcome a chance to fight the man.

Meservy's eyes glinted, but he didn't take the bait. "I have no redskin squaw in the forest, either."

There was silence around him for a moment. He glanced at the ladies behind Meservy, and to his astonishment saw faces that tried to appear horrified but eyes that glowed with something he did not recognise. The one thing he knew was that he was no match at this kind of talk with Meservy, so he shut up. He sought Sarah's eyes in the group around him, and was relieved when she smiled. There seemed to be an unspoken understanding between them, an intimacy that was above the kind of pettiness exhibited by John Meservy. Sarah came up to him and said, "You are really marvellous, Dan. All Baltimore will be agog by to-morrow."

It gave him a warm glow to know that Sarah was pleased, but something impelled him to look over the heads of the ladies, and he saw John Meservy watching them. Meservy turned away immediately, but not soon enough to hide the fact that he was jealous.

That was a shock to Dan, but he knew a way to take care of it. When he and Sarah alighted from the coach before the Radnor house that night, he took her hand as the coach rolled off, and held her for a moment. She looked up at him in the moonlight and asked slyly, "Is there something you want to say, Dan?"

What he really wanted was to know how she felt in his arms. He started to raise his hands, but then the difference between them overcame him, and he stepped back.

But she moved towards him, and stood almost touching him. "Yes, Dan?"

His arms went around her, and she came still closer until her warm body was against his. Her head was back, and he kissed her on the lips. Her small hands clung fiercely to his upper arms.

Finally he took a deep breath. "Miss," he said, "I'm asking you to marry me."

"Dan!"

"You aren't very big for heavy work," he said; "but I think we can make out."

"You're surely not serious."

"I surely am, ma'am."

"Well, I . . ."

He was amused to see her lose the poise she had maintained so naturally all night. And it endeared her to him to find that she was not always sure of herself.

"There's no use waitin', ma'am. There's land up in Wyoming Valley to be had for the taking. We can build up a mighty nice farm."

"But, Dan! The Indians!"

"We've taken care of them so far," he reminded her.

She withdrew with seeming reluctance. "I don't . . . you . . . we don't do things so precipitously in Baltimore," she said. "Mr. Meservy has been courting me for months. Do you think this is fair to him?"

Dan answered coldly, "I am not concerned with what is fair to an unmannered man like Meservy. If you are not already spoken for, and if you will consider marriage with me, I will speak to your father."

He thought there was promise in her voice when she said, "Father is asleep now. You cannot see him until to-morrow."

He felt himself singing with joy as he took off his hunting-shirt and got into bed. Perhaps they didn't do things that fast in Baltimore. They lived a life of leisure and they could afford to play at life. But on the frontier a man never knew whether he would be alive to-morrow. Life was to be lived and not wasted, and waiting until to-morrow might waste it all. Indeed they did do things differently. They had a wilderness to take away from the Indians, to turn into farms and homes; they had families to raise and grandchildren to watch out for, and it behoved any serious-minded man to let no grass grow under his feet.

He blew out the candle that must have been lighted by a servant, and lay down. It was none of his responsibility that Meservy had so far delayed asking Sarah the question. Meservy was a scoundrel anyway; Georgina's experience was proof of that.

Meservy might yet challenge him to a duel. Dan grinned in the darkness. That would give him the right to name the weapons, and he had no fear of meeting Meservy on an even basis.

CHAPTER
NINE

He was up early the next morning. The household was still, and he went quietly outside. The groom had already fed the horses, and they were munching oats and stamping in their stalls, switching their tails and scratching their sides against the thick boards.

"It's a good horse you-all got, mister," said the groom.

"He doesn't look like much, but he's got bottom," said Dan.

"Ah'll clip him down if you-all want me to, suh."

"Better not try it," Dan advised. "That horse is skitterish when you get around his legs."

"All right, boss, ah won't bother him with the shears — but how about lettin' him run with the othahs?"

"That'll be all right; he won't give any trouble."

The negro blacksmith was building up a fire in his forge; the harness-maker, an old, white-haired black, sat outside in the morning sun and smoked a corncob pipe. Dan found the cabin where the cooking was done at a huge fireplace hung with kettles and pots. He looked in the wagon shed, where two carriages and three wagons and a regular stage coach were kept. He saw black mammies chasing children off to the vegetable garden with baskets and hoes and much automatic scolding. "You-all bring back plenty of strawbarries or the boss be ready to give you a whalin'.'"

He investigated the root cellar, with walls lined with sacks of white potatoes, sweet potatoes, carrots, pumpkins, and squash. He walked across the fine grass where the horses ran, and noted that they had half a section to themselves. There was a small stream running through the field, and it was as pretty as a picture: deep grass, cold water, and no Indians.

When he got back to the whitewashed fence and climbed through it, there was activity at the big house. He went in the back door, and the maid said, "You-all bettah git ready for breakfast, suh."

He went upstairs, tossed his coon-skin cap under the bed, washed his face and hands, and came down.

Theophilus Radnor was not an old man but he had worry-lines that belonged to an old man. He was portly, and he wore black mutton-chops and a fringe of chin whiskers that was beginning to turn grey.

"I wanted to talk to you, Mr. Radnor."

Theophilus waved it away with a pudgy hand. "Not now, Dan. Not now, I never mix business with breakfast. That's the one time of the day I don't give any attention to anything but food — and you'll find there's plenty of that: ham, bacon, biscuits, butter and honey, coffee and chocolate, melon — everything that's in season and some things that aren't. I dare say you don't have meals like this in the valley more than once a year."

88

"We have food," Dan said, "but not much variety. We can't depend on gardens, for the Indians raid them. Sometimes they raid our smoke-houses too, so a lot of our food comes from the forest. There's usually plenty of it, but there may be only one thing at a time."

"Such as what?" asked Sarah.

He looked at her, visioning her in a cabin of their own.

"We shoot a deer or a bear or find a wild honey tree, and we eat all we want until it's gone."

"Sounds improvident to me," said Theophilus.

"It isn't really. It's just practical. Meat doesn't keep for ever. We eat it and then look for more. The forest is full of game."

He rode to the warehouse in the carriage with Theophilus. They negotiated the narrow, crooked streets — some paved with cobblestones which made far rougher riding than on the worst-gaited old plough-horse in Pennsylvania — and turned down towards the docks. Theophilus sent the carriage back home. "He'll pick us up for supper."

He led the way into his office in one corner of the warehouse, hung his hat on a peg and sat in a rawhide-bottomed chair. "Now, Dan'l, what's on your mind? Want to borrow money?"

"Not exactly," said Dan. "I want to *spend* some money."

Theophilus grunted. He was turning over some bills of lading, and didn't seem at all astonished. "What do you want to buy?"

"Some of the goods that have been on the lists we've been getting back unfilled."

Theophilus didn't look up. "I suspected as much." He picked up the sheafs of paper and bounced them on one edge until they were neatly square with one another. "Can't fill orders unless I have the goods," he said.

Dan frowned. "You . . ."

The outer door opened. A cheery voice said, "Good day, Theophilus," and a slight, wiry, sandy-haired man bounced in.

"Good day, Pat," Theophilus said heavily.

The slight man glanced at Dan.

"Customer of ours," Theophilus said. "A dissatisfied customer." He got up and waddled across to the clerk's desk and laid down the bills of lading, then came back. "Pat, this is Dan'l Shankle. You heard of him, fightin' Indians in Wyoming Valley."

"Begorrah, yes!" The sandy-haired man shook hands. "It's Patrick Evers I am, at your service."

"Dan'l," said Theophilus, "Mr. Evers here is the biggest merchant in Baltimore, and he has as much cause as you to complain about the scarcity of goods." He sat down again. "In fact," he said wearily, "he does complain."

"I was told you had a ship unloading yesterday," said Evers.

Theophilus sighed. "The ladings are over there — such as they are. Twenty barrels of rum, half a dozen hogsheads of sugar, a few cases of iron articles, three hundred bolts of cotton goods from India, forty

90

bundles of dried cowhides, twenty-six cases of corks, sixty-two sacks of aniseed, four casks of roll brimstone and twelve hundred pounds of liquorice root. Twelve hundred pounds!" he said disgustedly. "When am I going to get something I can sell?"

"More to the point," said Evers, "when are you going to get something *I* can sell?"

"Do I understand that you are not getting goods?" asked Dan.

Theophilus looked sadly at Evers. "You both come with me," he said, and led them into the outer warehouse. It was vast — and it was empty. Theophilus shook his head. "We get a driblet of goods now and then, like the bills I just showed you, but we are getting almost nothing we can sell to the consumer. Who wants twelve hundred pounds of liquorice root?"

Their footsteps echoed hollowly in the emptiness of the big building. They reached the end and saw the small piles of goods represented by the bills.

Dan frowned. "Why aren't you getting goods? It isn't a matter of credit, is it?"

"My credit's as good as the Bank of England. It's a question of getting the merchandise. We order it, but I am not receiving it, and no one else in Baltimore is getting any more than I am. According to the post, importers in other towns are in the same position. We get small consignments of scattered merchandise, but the big shipments of manufactured goods that come from England — those do not arrive."

"How about rifles?" asked Dan.

"Rifles are the most difficult of all." Theophilus led them back to his office. "During this past winter four shiploads of goods, all containing large quantities of firearms, have disappeared on the high seas, supposedly captured by pirates."

"It's the King's fault!" Evers exclaimed. "He and his infernal profit-minded merchants!"

"That's hardly so," said Theophilus. "Eventually we find these cargoes are cleared for Baltimore as they should be. But they don't reach port — and I'm sitting here with nothing to sell. I'll go bankrupt if this keeps up."

Evers laughed. "You'll be in business long after the rest of us have closed our doors. Theophilus," he said to Dan, "has a finger in every pie in Baltimore."

But Dan, sitting there, was getting angry. He got on his feet. "While you two gentlemen are worrying about a profit," he said, "men and women and children on the western frontier are depending on rifles and powder to save their hair from the Indians. We can use animal skins for clothing. We can kill our meat and raise our own corn and mill our own wheat. We can dress out logs to build a house. But we have got to get manufactured goods from the cities. Have you ever," he demanded, "seen the Indians burn a man alive?"

Theophilus looked up, intent. Patrick Evers was temporarily speechless.

"I have," said Dan. "Along with Tom Cotlow, I was captured by Captain Pipe's Delawares. They stripped him and painted him black and tied him with a long rope and built fires all around him, so he could never get away from the heat. The wood was hickory, and it burns hot. His shrieks will live in Pennsylvania for eternity."

"And you —"

"They tied me to the same stake with the same rope, but a rescue party came from the valley." He paused. "Now you know why I fought for his widow, Mrs. Cotlow, and you know why it isn't a thing I remember with any pleasure — fighting for a woman whose husband was killed that way."

"I know that life on the frontier is difficult," Theophilus began, "but —"

"There are no buts," Dan said harshly. "You live or you die. And living depends to a large extent on getting manufactured goods — particularly rifles — from men like you. The Indians get rifles from the British. They have better firearms than we." He stared uncompromisingly at Theophilus. "Is that where our rifles go — to the Indians?"

Theophilus shook his head. "Not to my knowledge, though I don't know for certain where they do go. They don't come to me, and I have not been able to determine why."

"Don't you have gunsmiths?" Evers asked Dan.

"Not enough. We have depended on imports. We have few gunsmiths and almost no equipment. To get equipment we would have to depend again on imports."

"Rifles are at a premium all over America," said Theophilus. "In Kentucky a good rifle will bring thirty dollars. In New Spain, if you smuggle rifles past the border, you can get twice that, in gold or horses or slaves."

"Is that why we aren't getting them?" Dan asked sharply.

"Again, I don't know."

"It's probably because the damned Tories are turning them over to the Indians," Evers said hotly.

Theophilus shook his head. "I don't agree with that. I'm loyal to the Crown, and I see no reason for this talk of rebellion."

"I said nothing of rebellion," Evers retorted.

"Rebellion is talked everywhere," Theophilus insisted, "and your words reflect it."

Evers's face was red. "Good day, Theophilus," he said, and stalked out with as much indignation as a little man could demonstrate.

Dan had cooled off a little. "Mr. Radnor, isn't there anybody else in Baltimore who has rifles?"

Theophilus sighed heavily. "Not to my knowledge," he said. "But to satisfy yourself, I suggest you inquire. You might try Robinson or Morris & Draper. They probably would have arms or information if anybody has. But don't take my word alone. Ask at any place that strikes your fancy." He rubbed his whiskers. "Though it is not a question of life or death for us as merchants, it is still a serious problem. Our living depends on the goods we have to sell."

Dan walked down the dock to a painted sign that said, "Alf. Robinson, Importer."

Robinson was a tall man with penetrating blue eyes. He watched Dan as he talked. Then he got up and said, "Come with me."

They walked into the big warehouse, and their footsteps echoed hollowly in a huge empty space.

"You see," said Robinson, "a small assortment of goods on the open dock. That was unloaded this morning from the brigantine *Jonathan*. I got this much from the shipload. The other importers along the dock will get about the same and, as you can see, it is pitifully small. We are not getting a tenth of the goods necessary to supply the town of Baltimore.

"What can we do, then, in Wyoming Valley?"

"There is only one answer known to me: find out where the big shipments are going."

"How can a man do that?"

"I don't know."

CHAPTER
TEN

Dan spent the rest of the morning looking at empty warehouses. He reached the end of the docks and went across the street for a glass of grog. He was just stepping inside when he was hailed. "Dan Shankle!"

Dan stopped, turned, and scowled.

John Meservy came up the street towards him, picking his way through the dust with his silver-buckled shoes. "I'll stand you a treat of rum," he said.

Dan looked at Meservy's fancy clothes and made no attempt to hide his distaste.

"Oh, come," said Meservy. "You needn't take offence. I am as accustomed to leather clothing as you are, but I live in Baltimore and dress as Baltimoreans do. Come on in with me."

They went in, Meservy ordered Jamaica rum. It was the best, and it was not for children, but he noted that Meservy tossed it off like water. "What's your business?" asked Dan.

"Broker," said Meservy. "The only difference between Theophilus and me is that he orders from England or France or India, and resells, while I take my chances and pick up what I can. If an importer finds himself overstocked, on firearms, for instance, I take them off his hands. He has certain outlets for his goods, on which he depends for the bulk of his imports. It is my business to have other outlets. I am a sort of balance for the importer, you might say."

Dan had heard only one word. "Do you have any rifles now?"

Meservy laughed disdainfully. "More rum," he ordered. "Nobody has rifles." He sneered. "You're a fool for even thinking you can find rifles — in Baltimore or anywhere else."

"Why so?"

"The importers, merchants — all are working for the King, and they don't get rifles because the British War Office fears a rebellion. They are afraid to put rifles into the hands of the colonists for fear they'll be turned against His Majesty's soldiers."

Dan fingered his glass. "Maybe I'd do better in New York."

"It's worse in New York," Meservy said. "The only place to solve your problem is in England."

Dan pushed back the second glass of rum. "I serve notice," he said. "I am going to find out where these rifles are going and who is responsible for it. When I put my anger on the man, I will break him in two."

Meservy watched him coolly. "Before you do anything precipitate," he said, "it might be well to remember that the other man will have something to say about that."

"Marse Shankle," said a voice at Dan's elbow.

Dan looked up at the groom. "Yes?"

"Missy Sarah done send me to find you, suh."

Dan felt the alertness of the frontier come over him. "Is there trouble?"

"No, suh. I don't think so, suh. Missy Sarah done tell me to fetch you, suh."

Meservy downed his drink. "You might as well mind Sarah. She always gets what she wants."

Dan didn't answer. After all, he was her guest. "I'll come," he said, and went outside.

He was let off at the ornate front door. Sarah met him in the hallway, cool, fragrant, skin dusky-white. She had to tip her head far back to look at him. "There is another reception to-night by the Misses Blakesley, and they have especially requested that you attend, and by all means wear your frontier uniform." She smiled beguilingly.

"It's not a uniform," he said stiffly. "It's what we wear — because it's all we have."

She patted his arm. For a little girl, he thought, she was amazingly confident. "Did you speak to my father this morning?"

"No. I've been trying to get rifles."

"Are rifles important?"

"They come ahead of food."

"Well, I'm sure father can manage some. Is it true that you use the rifles to kill Indians?"

"Indians and meat."

"How many Indians have you killed?"

Her inquisitiveness unexpectedly bothered him. "I never kept track," he said. "When the Indians crowd us, we shoot to keep 'em back. When they try to sneak in on you, you have to kill them. There isn't time to count."

"You keep the . . . scalps, you said."

He thought her eyes were over-bright. "We don't always scalp them. They take away their dead when they can. Scalps aren't important anyway. We do it because the Indians do it."

She clung to his forearm with both hands. "Tell that to the ladies to-night," she said.

It was midnight when they got home, but to his astonishment he found Theophilus stretched out before the open fireplace in a small room opposite the parlour. It was a cool evening, and Theophilus was toasting his shins and sipping a glass of brandy.

Dan kissed Sarah good night and went into the library. "There's something else I want to talk to you about, sir," said Dan.

"I'll talk first," said Theophilus. "But sit down. You're too damned tall."

Dan sat in a big leather chair that was nothing like the highly decorative chairs in the parlour. He was able to lean back while Theophilus poured brandy in a big-bowled glass. Dan took it and stretched his long legs towards the fire.

"You people in Wyoming Valley," said Theophilus, "are not the only ones concerned with shortages of goods — especially rifles. You saw how Patrick Evers stalked out this morning."

"Yes, sir."

"Evers is an excellent chap, but his feeling is typical of the turmoil in the colonies to-day. Most of us know that we are discriminated against by the Crown, but we feel also that the position of the colonists at such a distance from the mother country is a situation that has to be worked out gradually. There are many men among us who foster discontent and suspicion to serve their own ends. They work behind closed doors and hide their true intent behind smiling masks." Theophilus sighed. "It is interesting to note that in most cases these men are serving their own personal ends. They have no interest in the colonies or their people."

Dan sipped his brandy, thinking immediately of Meservy. Was Meservy one of those of whom Theophilus was speaking?

"Take the matter of rifles," Theophilus went on. "I place orders for all of the Watts firearms, and all of the output is consigned to me, but they do not reach me. What does happen to them is fairly common knowledge."

Dan looked at him sharply. "What is that?"

"They are routed to New Spain and sold at an immense profit — not by me or by any legitimate importer or broker in Baltimore."

"Meaning what?" asked Dan.

"There is in town a man who seemingly does nothing but always has plenty of money. He dresses well and drives a fine carriage. He has plenty of slaves and a stable of blooded horses. We do not know where he gets his money."

"Do you think this man is diverting the cargoes either by piracy or bribery, and selling the goods in the Spanish colonies?"

Theophilus poured them both a second glass of brandy. "We know the Spanish are starving for goods — much more so than you are. The Spanish colonial administration is far more bungling than the British, and they are afraid to give the colonists weapons to protect themselves. So, since there is a relative plenty of gold and silver in that country, goods bring extremely high prices."

"To be perfectly frank," said Dan, "what is to prevent legitimate importers and brokers from diverting such goods?"

"The fact that our business are built up in Baltimore; our homes and families are here; most of us have large estates here. We must continue to furnish goods to our merchants in this town if we are to stay here — and most of us are too old to go to a new country and face the hazards of the frontier. We are not young and vigorous like you, Dan."

Dan held the brandy before the firelight. "Eventually won't these ships and their masters have to be accounted for?"

"'Eventually' is a long time. If these cargoes are being diverted to the West Indies — which includes all of New Spain — it would be very difficult to trace them down within an ordinary lifetime." He rotated the glass in his pudgy fingers. "With the Spaniards restricting trade on every hand, even among Spanish colonies, there is a great deal of contraband trade going on. There are restrictions, heavy taxes, and a downright shortage of goods from the Spanish mainland. Nor can the Spanish Government assure delivery. Sometimes the colonies down there go for three or four years without a single shipload of goods — and of what use are gold and silver if you cannot spend it? On top of all this, there is piracy. Not only are the seas filled with pirate ships and villainous crews who think nothing of sinking a ship and appropriating her cargo, but there are countless ships carrying letters of marque from some neutral country, and these, too, are hard to control."

"I don't know about that, sir."

"A ship of some neutral country can stop a ship of British registry, for instance, and, finding contraband goods, confiscate it and proceed to a Spanish port where the goods are turned in, and the capturing ship is awarded a percentage of the haul."

"It seems to open up abuses."

"It certainly does. Some crews stop the Spanish ships themselves, murder the crews, sink the ships, and destroy the papers. Then with a little bribery the goods are passed through the Spanish Customs and sold at a healthy profit for all save the original consigners."

Dan drank his brandy.

"Nor is that the whole story," said Theophilus, staring into the fire. "British, French, and Dutch ships prey constantly on the Spanish merchantmen with impunity. There are treaties, but what are treaties?"

"It seems to me that a more or less regular disappearance of ships from one trade route does indicate an organised effort."

"Correct. It also indicates an organised method of disposal."

"What is the name of the man you mentioned?" said Dan.

Theophilus looked at him obliquely and poured them a third glass of brandy. "A man who, I am sorry to say, has asked for the hand of my daughter — John Meservy. I believe you met him last night."

Dan sat back. "Uh . . . yes."

"You're a man who is alive because of your ability to size up other men. What do you think of Meservy?"

Dan's brows moved together. "It is hardly fitting for me to give an opinion of my rival."

Theophilus glanced up. "You, too, eh? That makes an even dozen in the last twelve months."

"But Sarah —"

"Encouraged you, no doubt." He reached the fire tongs and pushed a small log into the centre of the fire. "She might have meant it, of course. Sarah's a wilful girl. She gets what she wants — and she might want you."

"Would you give your consent, sir?"

"If Sarah wants it, but I don't like the idea of her going up into Pennsylvania when you haven't got rifles to protect her."

"Then it is true you are not able to furnish rifles?"

Theophilus thumped his glass on the table. "Why do you think I spent the morning showing you my empty warehouse?"

"Sorry, sir." He finished the brandy. "Were those rifles on the *Matilda* dated?"

"Watts always dates his rifles. They'd show 1772."

"Then they could be identified?"

"I'd think so. Since I contracted for his entire output, if I found a Watts rifle with that date, I'd feel certain it had come from the *Matilda*."

Dan moved restlessly. "Under the circumstances, it would not only help us on the frontier, but it might remove a source of trouble in the colonies, if we could find out who is responsible. If those rifles could be found in the New Philippines, for instance —"

"If you can find who is behind it," Theophilus said, "there will be less likelihood of war between England and the colonies."

"Could Meservy benefit from such a war?"

"It adds to the general confusion. He can pirate cargoes and sell them at exorbitant prices to those who cannot afford to haggle. That is just one of many ways he can profit."

Dan stood up to the full height of his six-feet-four. "The crops are in," he said. "I will go to New Orleans to-morrow."

"Do you know anybody down there?"

"Simon Jeffreys, who grew up with me in Virginia."

"What is his business?"

Dan smiled. "He is supposed to be running a blacksmith's shop, but he's probably as deep in some kind of shady business as a man could be and stay out of jail."

"You think you can depend on him?"

"If anybody would know things like that, Simon would. And I would trust him with my life."

"It would be helpful to have a contact."

"If we find the rifles," Dan said confidently, "we can backtrack them and find the man who was responsible for their getting to New Spain."

Theophilus considered. "It will be dangerous."

"No more so than the Senecas."

Theophilus considered. "I'd suggest you enter at Manchac."

Dan smiled. "I'll take a load of contraband goods and go trading myself."

"That would require money, Dan."

"I've got a little."

"I'll give you more," Theophilus said abruptly. "If you make a profit, we'll divide half and half. If you find out about the rifles, you'll be doing the colonies a service."

"I'm —"

"No argument, young man. You've been doing business with me for a long time, and I'm willing to gamble on you. There's a sloop, the *Rebecca*, sixty-five tons, sailing with the tide to-morrow for Pensacola with a cargo of flour, whisky, and fish. I'm quite sure it is destined eventually for the Tejas country, for Florida is British now, you know, and a great quantity of English goods enters at Pensacola, finds its way into West Florida, and enters Louisiana at Little Manchac. Once admitted, it is fairly simple. It goes up the Mississippi to the Red River of Natchitoches and follows that stream into New Spain, or it goes on up to the Arkansa River and enters by the route of the *contrabandistas*. Of the two, Natchitoches is the easier but the Arkansa is the more profitable. At any rate, a trader would not be permitted to take rifles through Natchitoches, and so it seems to leave the Arkansa Post as the point of entry. Since I am gambling anyway, I may as well gamble on that. I would say to go by the Arkansa River and make for the Wichita villages."

"If I am to leave in the morning, I won't have time to buy trade goods . . ."

"I doubt if you could find enough here, anyway. Wait until you reach Little Manchac. The English traders have more contraband there than we have honest goods here."

"Very well, sir. I'll be on the *Rebecca*."

"You'll need money. Trade goods comes roughly to two thousand dollars a ton, and you might as well take enough to show a profit. I'll send my black with a letter of credit for twelve hundred pounds to the captain of the sloop, and you'll get it from him. You can draw on it in Pensacola, for I have associates there."

Dan took a full breath. "Thank you, sir."

"Don't thank me. I may be sending you to your death. The *contrabandistas* are bad ones."

"I'm sure they are no worse than Captain Pipe's Delawares."

"You would be a fool to count too heavily on that." Theophilus got up. He was a small man, Dan now realised, not much taller than Sarah. Dan shook hands. "I'll be back," he said, "with news."

Theophilus looked worried. "I wish you godspeed," he said. "And by the way . . . John Meservy left Baltimore by stage this afternoon, headed for Richmond, supposedly."

106

Dan left with the glow of the brandy in his blood and the heady vigour of impending action in his brain. A lighted candle was on a table in the hall. He picked it up and started upstairs, but Sarah came from somewhere and stood in his path. "You've been talking to father?"

"Yes," he said, wondering if her exotic hair and eyes could possibly be any lovelier.

"I'm happy," she said, lowering her eyes. "To-morrow I'll send you to a tailor who will provide suitable clothes, and you —"

"Suitable clothes for what?"

Her eyes widened. "Your uniform is distinctive, but of course you can't wear it in town indefinitely. You will have to —"

"I'm not going to be in town indefinitely," he said, and his voice was more harsh than he intended. "I'm leaving in the morning for Louisiana."

Dan finished his story and reached for his carrot of tobacco. "You know the rest."

"Somewhat," said Simon. "You came to my blacksmith's shop and accused me of using it as a front for contraband activities. I swore on my sacred honour that it wasn't so because I didn't have enough money to finance smuggling, and then you offered me a job. So what could I do? The blacksmith business in New Orleans was slow anyway."

The two husky-bodied Wichita girls had filled the water-bags and apparently decided to take a swim, for they had shed their grass skirts and were playing in the shallow water, giggling and chattering like magpies.

"So now," Simon said thoughtfully, "you want to find some rifles with 'Wm. Watts 1772,' stamped on them, and they may be in those long boxes over there under that cottonwood tree."

Dan took a deep breath. "Yes," he said.

"How do you figure to look at them?"

"He brought them here to trade. Pretty soon an Indian will have one of those rifles." He bit off a chew with his strong white teeth. "When he does, it's only a matter of time until I'll have a look at it."

CHAPTER
ELEVEN

Poeyfarré came from Eyasiquiche's place, his square frame abounding with energy. He sat down and rolled a cigarette and lit it from the fire. "Everybody stick close to-night," he said, "and keep your eyes open, for the Spanish may be trailing thees man."

"What's his name?" asked Dan.

Poeyfarré said pointedly, "I do not know what hees name really is."

"You've seen him before?"

Poeyfarré glanced up. "I have see' him on two-three othair trips. He is well known in these villages."

"Where did he come from?"

"He has a trading licence but not for rifles. He probably came through Natchitoches to get the licence while the rifles were shipped to the Tejas coast, and he picked them up later."

"I never heard of him," Simon observed.

"Is possible. He may use a different name in different places. Anyhow, it's time to watch out. There weel be some throats cut around here before this is over."

He finished his cigarette and tossed the butt into the fire. He got up and went back to the chief's hut. Menard came from somewhere and lay on his side by the fire, which, in the twilight, looked nothing more than a pile of grey ashes.

Meservy passed them, going towards the centre of the village with an arm around each of the Wichita girls.

Dan watched him go into a hut with them, and looked back at the goods now piled under an oak tree. "Two men left to guard the stuff," he noted. "He doesn't trust the Wichitas."

"Or you," said Simon.

About dark the squaws began carrying up wood and building a big fire in the centre of the village. "We might as well go up and see what's on for supper," said Simon.

The slender Menard said, "Best we eat all we can now. It may be a long day to-morrow."

Two big pots of stew had been simmering all day, and Dan strongly suspected that most of the meat was dog.

"Nothing wrong with that," said Simon. "A young puppy is good eating."

Poeyfarré came over. "There is going be a heap big dance and celebration to-night. You men have a chance to make some friends — and maybe to-morrow thees man's goods don' hurt us so much."

Menard said, "I'm do' all I can, but I'm scare' there is too many girls for even a man like Menard."

"I'll back you up," said Simon.

"And you, Shankle . . ."

"I'll be on hand," Dan said.

He ate plentifully of the stew, and he had to admit it was good, whatever was in it. The young squaws were everywhere, looking expectant, but Dan left the fire and kept an eye on the goods under the oak tree. He wanted just one chance to look in those long boxes. If he should find what he suspected, he could then have a showdown with Meservy.

He went back to the hut where he could keep an eye on Meservy's guards. The two men sat on opposite sides of the tree with rifles across their legs. They weren't even drinking, Dan noted with some discouragement. The worst of it was, it was none of his business if Meservy *was* contrabanding rifles — unless those rifles were those intended for Wyoming Valley.

He sat there in the dark for quite a while, but always he kept an eye on the man guarding the long boxes. They talked to each other from time to time in low tones. They got up occasionally and walked around, but they stayed within arm's length of the tree and the boxes.

Simon returned along towards midnight. He sat down beside Dan and stretched. "It might not be such a bad life to settle down with the Wichitas, if a man could have the squaw he wanted."

"Couldn't you?"

Simon sighed. "She'd cost me too many mules." He yawned and went inside. Dan heard him settling down in the straw.

A couple of hours later the party had tapered off around the big fire, which was nothing more than a heap of glowing coals. Menard came back to the hut.

Dan cast a glance towards the tree. The moon was up and one of the guards was walking down towards the river. Dan got up and went quietly that way.

He came up behind the remaining man and smelled whisky, and knew the guards had been drinking on the sly. He looked towards the river. The first guard was not in sight. He backed off far enough to find a section of fallen limb green enough to use as a club. Then he returned to the tree.

The guard looked up just as Dan raised the club, and Dan caught him across the forehead. The man grunted and then toppled.

Dan let him sprawl on the ground. He stepped over him, picked up one of the long boxes, and started for his own lodge with the box held in both arms.

He stumbled over the club he had dropped, and went half-way to the ground. At that moment something thudded against the box, and he heard the whine of a quivering knife. He dropped the box and reached for his tomahawk.

Dan loosed the hatchet and felt it slide back into its rawhide loop.

"Pardon me," said Meservy's cynical voice. "I thought somebody was trying to steal my rifles." He stepped into the moonlight from the side of a meat-drying rack. "I didn't know it was you Shankle."

"You know it now."

"Just drop that tomahawk where it is. I'm holding a pistol on you."

Meservy came over and worked his knife out of the wood. That knife would have buried itself in Dan's chest if he had not stumbled. Meservy stood up, still holding the pistol on him. The guard groaned and rolled over.

A step sounded behind Dan. "Trouble?" asked Simon.

Meservy said to Dan, "Both of you go on back and mind your business. I've had you watched from the time I got here."

Dan had to accept it, although if he could catch Meservy off guard . . .

But the man knew what he was thinking. He backed up. "Get out of my camping ground and stay out. The next time I won't miss."

Dan and Simon went back. Simon slowly put his pistol away, saying nothing. Dan was chagrined, but there was nothing he could do. He got his blanket from the drying-rack, went inside and bedded down in the middle of the floor.

The sun was high when he awoke. He got his flint and steel and a piece of charred linen. He went outside and built a nest of dry twigs and got on his knees to work at the flint. The fire flamed up. He got the coffee pot and started for the river. The way led by the oak tree where the guards had been. They weren't there now, nor were the rifles.

He halted for a moment, assimilating this knowledge. Then he went to the river, washed out the pot and scoured it with sand, filled it half-full of sparkling water, and went back.

One fact was fairly obvious: those were the Watts rifles for which he was looking. Otherwise there was no point in guarding them; the presence of the boxes made it obvious that rifles were a part of Meservy's trade goods. The big question was: where had the rifles gone?

Poeyfarré came out of a grass hut, rubbed his eyes, looked towards Dan, and then came over to wait for the coffee.

"Those rifles disappeared this morning," Dan said.

Poeyfarré didn't look happy. "He's already sell his stuff, but don' worry. He weel have to take his pay in buffalo robes and deerskins — maybe some gold and silver. Thees fine metals have not come through a Crown smelter and are subject to fifty per cent tax."

"How about horses and mules?"

"De Mézières is very strict." Poeyfarré shook his head. "We can still make some good deals. The Camanche' have got to get rid of the mules and slaves they get by raiding the Spanish settlements and Apache villages."

"Why don't we trade directly with the Camanches?"

"It's safer to trade with the Wichitas," said Poeyfarré. "Anyhow, we can' get close enough to trade. They were camp' upstream last night, but they didn' even come in to have some dog stew because they don' trust anybody."

"Then they're waiting for what the Wichitas get from us?"

Poeyfarré stared at the oak tree under which there was nothing. "A bunch of Wichitas left this morning to take his stuff to the Camanches, and we'll have to wait until they get back — maybe to-night, maybe to-morrow night. There'll be powwows and pipe

114

smoking, and lots of argument over how many squaws a good rifle is worth."

"To-morrow," said Dan, pouring coffee into tin cups. "That's a long time to wait, especially when we're here without trading licences."

"You can't push 'em. Time doesn't mean anything to an Indian. And old Eyasiquiche is a sharp trader. He wants to be sure how much he's getting from the Camanches before he loads up too much goods."

"What do we do in the meantime?"

"Loaf, visit. You talk Wichita?"

"No."

"It's a good time to learn," he said, business-like. "I'll send one of Bird Running's daughters to teach you. You'll learn in wan beeg hurry."

Dan got up. This constant temptation was making him wonder why exactly he felt obligated to Sarah. Now that he thought about it, she hadn't even promised — except by implication, with her lips — which was a pretty good way to imply as he thought about it now. He looked at Poeyfarré a long time without seeing him, and finally he got up and said, "I think I'll take a ride around the village."

Poeyfarré's eyes were penetrating. "Take Simon with you. It isn't safe for one man to roam around this country alone."

Dan got up. "Where do you figure the other man's rifles went to?" He looked towards the oak tree.

Poeyfarré didn't hesitate. "To the Camanches, of course."

"Why did he sell so fast?" asked Simon. "I thought there was a bigger percentage if you took your time."

Poeyfarré frowned and looked again at the oak tree. "That has always been true. I do not un'erstand it."

But Dan thought he did. Meservy had wanted to get rid of those rifles before Dan somehow saw the name and date on them.

They found their mules grazing along the river. They saddled them and rode out to the south, over undulating prairie country with good grass.

From a high mound they watched Meservy's pack train wind east, back towards the Red River and Natchitoches.

"Mighty quick turnover for him," said Simon. "Big profit in that kind of business."

Dan said thoughtfully, "Do you think those rifles really went west?"

"Bound to," said Simon. "That's where the Camanches are, and where the Camanches are, that's where the money is in guns."

"That's an odd belt of timber to the east," Dan noted.

"They call that the Cross Timbers. Sandy soil, different kinds of oak, some elm and hickory. It's only three or four leagues wide and extends south past the Brazos, I hear, and north past the Canadian Fork."

It still lacked two hours of supper time when Dan saw movement in the Cross Timbers ahead of them. "Down!" he grunted.

They alighted on their moccasins and led the mules to lower ground.

"What was it?" asked Simon.

"It looked like the east end of a mule headed west."

Simon frowned. "Why would a mule be going west?"

Dan started to follow the bottom towards the timber. "That what I want to know."

They found out minutes later when a line of uniformed Spanish soldiers rode through an open spot in the timber. "Jumping Christopher!" whispered Simon. "No wonder your friend got out of here so fast. He knew the *soldados* were coming."

"How did he know it?"

"He probably paid the lieutenant to give him a day's warning." Simon was mounting his mule.

"We're in for it," Dan said.

"Not if we get to the village first. We'll stick to the edge of the Cross Timbers north a ways and then cut through. It's slower but it's shorter."

They went through the Cross Timbers at a trot. They turned north along the edge, but Simon was shaking his head. "He's not so dumb, that lieutenant. Once he got through the timber, he put spurs to his outfit."

Dan studied the ground as they loped north. The bent and bruised grass left a trail as plain as a wagon road. He moved alongside Simon. "Not much use hurrying. We couldn't go around them now."

"No, but I want to see the finish," said Simon.

They saw it. Eight Spanish soldiers with short *fusiles* or rifles, heavy blunderbusses, sabres, lances, and shields were standing at attention before their piles of goods.

117

CHAPTER
TWELVE

Dan rode up and alighted from his mule. Simon was beside him. "Who's in charge here?" asked Dan.

A swarthy young man stepped forward. His uniform, Dan thought, was in excellent shape for having come all the way from Nacogdoches or Béxar. Undoubtedly Simon was right: the Spanish cavalry had been camped about a day's march away, waiting for Meservy to return — and possibly waiting payment for being so considerate.

"You are English?" he asked.

"No," said Simon. "We're French."

The lieutenant looked incredulous. "Your names, please."

"Daniel Shankle."

The Spaniard sneered at him. "That's an English name."

He spun on Simon. "And your name, *señor?*"

Simon sighed. "Pierre Duval."

"You, too, look English."

The Spaniard's eyes narrowed. "*Bien*. Let me see your passports, *señores*."

Dan said steadily, "We have no passports."

Lieutenant Borica's eyes flashed. "Without passports — both of you?"

"Both."

Borica showed great satisfaction now. "And your licences to trade?"

"We didn't know we had to have a licence," said Simon, wide-eyed. "We just brought in some ordinary trade goods, to try to pick up some deer skins and buffalo robes. We —"

"*¡Silencio!* This is your goods?" Borica asked. "This many piles of goods?"

"Sure, that's ours," said Dan. "You want to look through it?"

"Is not necessary, *señor*. I take possession of it all in the name of His Most Catholic Majesty."

But Eyasiquiche pushed his huge bulk through the Spanish soldiers. "*¿Que hay?*" he demanded.

Borica explained in Spanish. "These two men have no passports, no licences, but they bring trade goods into Tejas. I have confiscated their goods."

Eyasiquiche answered promptly, in Spanish almost as good as Borica's, and Dan's respect for the Wichita went up.

"They are my guests," Eyasiquiche said. "It is not a hospitable thing you do, to take the belongings of my guests."

Dan watched them. Eyasiquiche was a smart Indian, all right. He knew that if word got around at Arkansa Post that the Wichitas had let a few Spanish soldiers come in and confiscate trade goods, there would be trouble with the *contrabandistas*. Probably they would

119

bypass the Wichitas altogether, and certainly Eyasiquiche did not want that.

Dan began to feel encouraged.

Borica also saw which way the wind was blowing. He watched the Indian with narrowed eyes. "There are regulations," he muttered.

A second Indian came forward, a smaller and older man with a crippled leg. "You will listen to One-Horned Buffalo," he said, and the camp went suddenly quiet. "I am an old man and I take little part in these squabbles of children. But my heart is good towards the Spanish. I have made promises not to war upon the Spanish and not to take their women and children from San Antonio de Béxar, and I have kept those promises. Now," he said scornfully, "a lieutenant with eight soldiers comes into my village and tries to tell us what we can do and what we cannot do. I say this is our village and this has been a historic site of Toavayas tribes since before I can remember." His old eyes were filled with fire. "And now a young soldier, a boy who has had no chance to prove himself as a warrior, with eight miserable soldiers, comes into our village and insults our guests. Does not the great Spanish father value his friendship with the Wichitas enough to send a man with many medals to insult us?"

Borica was trapped and he knew it. He looked around at the ring of bronze-skinned Wichitas. They were muttering now, hostile-eyed, and Borica looked back at One-Horned Bull. He looked beyond the ring of warriors at the squaws.

Borica was trying to figure his way out, Dan knew. The Spaniard was in a bad spot. He didn't have enough men to start trouble, but he would lose face if he backed down.

"We have a great chief," he said finally, "as great as you, One-Horned Bull, and he gives me orders. I have to enforce them."

Now Poeyfarré, who must have been awaiting the proper moment, came forward. "Governor Rippedá has allowed this innocent trade to go on for three years," he said.

Borica turned to this new opponent. You had to hand it to the Spaniard, thought Dan; he wasn't afraid of the odds. "Who are you?" he demanded.

The Frenchman shrugged. "They call me Poeyfarré. I have trade' all over the Tejas country."

"You have no rifles?"

"*Certainement* no."

"You take mules and slaves in trade, though?"

"*Mais non*, of course not. Such a thing is unthinkable!"

Borica shifted his attack. "You have a passport?"

Poeyfarré shrugged. He was, Dan thought, enjoying the whole thing, because he, too, considered there was only one way for the lieutenant to get out alive if he insisted on sticking to the letter of the law.

"You have a licence to trade?"

"No," Poeyfarre admitted.

"Then I am forced to confiscate your goods also."

"But Rippedá . . ."

Borica said, his back like a ramrod, "I do not represent the governor of Tejas, *señor*. I represent Don Hugo Ocónor, the *comandante-inspector* whom one of your men mentioned. Don Hugo takes orders directly from the viceroy in Méjico, and does not serve His Majesty under the governor of Tejas."

Eyasiquiche and One-Horned Bull seemed temporarily nonplussed. Menard whispered in Dan's ear: "Ocónor! That's deeferent!"

Borica was barking orders at his men. They assumed positions around Dan's pile of goods, and Dan began to get his dander up. "I can take a tomahawk and wipe out the whole bunch," he growled.

"Best not be impulsive," said Menard. "Ocónor would send more soldiers."

Poeyfarré jerked his head at Dan. "We have wan beeg conference," he said.

"I guess so." Dan, Simon and Menard left the circle. Poupelinière and Brognard joined them, and Poeyfarré led the way to the centre of the village. "We are in beeg trouble," said the energetic Frenchman.

"I don't see any trouble we can't handle," said Dan. "There are six of us. We can lick nine Spaniards without pulling a knife. If we couldn't, what about the Wichitas?"

Poeyfarré seated himself, cross-legged, near the big kettle of stew that was always hanging over the fire before Eyasiquiche's lodge. "We could take care of Borica and his eight men, and not lose a scalp, but Borica represents Ocónor, and he's a bad hombre."

"The Wichitas . . ."

122

"They know Ocónor, too. All the Indians know him, and they call him *el Capitán Colorado*, not only because he is red-haired but because he is a very hard fighter and he never gives up. If he heard that Borica and his men were massacred he would probably follow us all back to the Arkansa and wipe out *El Cadrón*."

Dan frowned. "Everybody turns tail when Ocónor is mentioned! Well, I'm not afraid of him. Those goods represent *all* of my future and part of somebody else's."

"You can get it back," said Poeyfarré. "One good trip is all you need."

Eyasiquiche waddled up and sat down by the kettle.

Poeyfarré moved a little to make way for him. "What is your answer, great chief?"

Eyasiquiche's black eyes were quick and evasive. "We are great warriors. We have beaten the Spanish and we can beat them again. But we have lost many young men to the Osage. Numbers of our squaws are without men now. Should we then lose still more fighters over a pile of trade goods? This is an argument that can be settled peaceably. The Spanish officer does not back down. He is not afraid. One-Horned Bull says his medicine is very strong. We favour peace."

Borica was striding towards them. "You, Shankle —" (he had some trouble with the consonants at the end of the word) "and you, Poeyfarré, I am going to arrest for trading without a licence."

Poeyfarré stared at the lieutenant, and Dan knew the Frenchman had been pushed too far. He quietly punched Simon in the back.

But Eyasiquiche looked up at the Spaniard. "I do not think you need to arrest them," he said in Spanish.

Borica's eyebrows raised. "I have confiscated the goods," he said. "Now I am arresting the men who are responsible for it."

Eyasichique was unmoved. "You have confiscated the goods," he agreed; "but you are a long way from your soldiers now."

Borica stared at him. He looked back at the eight Spanish soldiers guarding the goods, and at the two hundred Wichita fighting men between himself and those eight. The Wichitas were armed with bows, and some had arrows against the strings; a few had rifles; nearly all had knives or lances.

Poeyfarré looked up and smiled. "You have make a tactical mistake, my friend'."

Borica swallowed, but he had a stiff back. "What do you propose to do?"

"You are the one who has been doing the proposing."

"What's the big Indian going to do?"

"I think it's plain where Eyasiquiche's interests lie. He doesn't care too much who gets the goods; his people will have them in the long run anyway. But arrest is going too far. It would get back to Arkansa Post, and the other traders would not come down here any more. They would instead trade guns to the Osages."

Borica said instantly, "That's exactly what we want to do — stop the *contrabandistas*!"

124

"You might," said Poeyfarré lazily; "but you might lose your life doing it. Now I'll offer a suggestion: you have confiscate' the goods and you have no use for them except to trade them to the Indians. Nobody will know how much there is or what you get for it. You can report to Ocónor that you took thees goods and give theem to the Wichitas because they are complaining for goods. So who knows if you sell a few of the horses and mules down along the Brazos? Is Hugo Ocónor watching everything?"

"I could not do that!"

"You not only could — but you would," said Poeyfarré. "Especially when you realise that these Wichitas are only going to let you go so far."

"What are you wishing to say?"

"We can take the loss of our goods once in a while," said Poeyfarré, "and we will — but we won't go back under arrest to rot in one of your stinking Spanish prisons."

"You mean there would be trouble?"

"Heap big trouble!"

Eyasiquiche nodded agreement.

"He knows," said Poeyfarré, "that the minute we stop coming down here we start selling rifles to the Osages — and Osages are heap bad medicine for the Wichitas."

Borica studied Poeyfarré, looked at Eyasiquiche, and glanced over the solid mass of Wichita warriors. Finally he said to Poeyfarré, "*Bien*. In the interest of peace I will not arrest you — but the next time it will not be so easy for you."

125

Poeyfarré grinned. "The next time," he said, "you better bring more soldiers."

Eyasiquiche looked up and grunted to the Wichitas. They moved back and made a path for Borica. He strode through, and the path closed behind him.

Poeyfarré got up and stretched. "So we are still free," he said.

"Sure," said Dan. "And out four thousand dollars worth of goods."

"We still have the mules."

"You may have some trouble getting them back to Arkansa Post," Dan said.

Poeyfarré got up, cat-like. "What does that mean?"

"I'm not going back," said Dan.

"Where you go, then?"

"West," said Dan. "I've got business with the Camanches."

Poeyfarré looked towards Borica, who was going on down to the river. "I'll have still more mules to take back," he said.

"You better make a deal with the Wichitas, then. I'm leaving for Camanche country in the morning."

"How many men are going with you?"

"I haven't asked."

"I'm going," said Simon. "I want to find out if a man can make any money trading with the Camanches instead of the Wichitas."

"I theenk I go too," said Menard.

"What's got into you fellows — going into Camanche country?"

"I want to see what it says on those rifles that came from Natchitoches," said Dan.

"I would not monkey with that Englishman. He's bad medicine."

"I don't need to see him. I want to talk to Toroblanco. All I need is to see one of those rifles."

Poeyfarré glared at Menard. "So what's got into you?"

Menard said lazily, "He'll need more than two — and I remember when he want' to help Chamillard and Dartigo."

Simon smoked a cigar that night. "Do you reckon there's any way your friend Meservy could do us any damage in Camanche country?"

"Not unless he's there himself."

"I don't figure there's any reason why he should be there." Simon frowned. "But I sure wouldn't put it past him."

CHAPTER
THIRTEEN

They were up long before daylight. Dan had made a deal with Poeyfarré to herd his extra mules back to Arkansa Post for half. "I'll be back for them," Dan said.

"I'm not sure we'll get through Osage country."

"With ten Wichita warriors, you'll get there. Anyway," said Dan, "you stand to make money by it. If I don't get back to Arkansa Post, you get all the mules."

But Poeyfarré was disturbed. "I don't know what you want to see those rifles for."

"I know," said Dan, "and it's a good reason. But I don't know why these other two are going."

Menard grinned. "You need some wan to speak the sign language . . . no?"

Simon looked up. "I'm goin' to see if I can make a couple of pesos. Maybe these here Camanches need a blacksmith."

They saddled the mules. The Wichita village was asleep; only the dogs were prowling among the lodges, hunting scraps of food. They had rifles, pistols, knives, and tomahawks; each had a pair of *alforjas* — one side filled with dried meat, the other with parched corn.

Poeyfarré still objected. "It ain't good sense," he said. "*Nobody* goes into Camanche country. There's no percentage in it."

"That's where you've got your saddle on backwards," Simon said, leaning over. "Didn't you ever wonder where all that silver comes from that doesn't have the royal stamp on it?"

"I've heard there are mines in Camanche country." Poeyfarré moved up and put his hand on the mule's neck. "You can't take it out, anyway. De Mézières would confiscate it."

Simon said mockingly, "Poeyfarré, you been in Louisiana long enough to know better than that. That's why you're takin' back a lot more mules than you brought with you."

The square man shrugged against the starlight. "All right. You know it all. I give you wan good wish: I hope they kill you quick and not slow." He slapped the mule on the rump. "Get out of here before Borica finds out. We'll tell him you got scared and went east."

"Thanks."

They pushed the mules hard, and by noon they had reached the mound. The river had abrupt banks of red clay and sandstone, and the current looked deep and sluggish.

They swam the stream about mid-afternoon, and Simon was worried. "I expected they'd have a watch around the mound," he said.

"If they want to attack, it would be easiest when we are in the water," Menard noted.

Dan was scanning the grass in all directions. "I don't see anything."

"You wouldn't see Camanches," said Simon.

"It's a funny feeling," said Dan, standing up in his saddle. "The country ought to be full of them. Maybe it is and maybe it isn't. If it isn't, where are they?"

They found out an hour later. The Camanche camp had been abandoned. They rode through it, surveying the refuse, while the mules fought their bits.

"Twenty-five or thirty lodges," Dan noted, "and they headed south-west. Let's go up a ways," he suggested, "and camp for the night. We'll figure out what's next to-morrow."

They went back to the Camanche camp-site and let the mules graze while they debated. Dan was strongly opposed to the others continuing with him. "I can do what I want to do by myself as well as with you fellows," he said earnestly.

"Don't you like our comp'ny?" asked Simon.

"You are both fine to ride with, but I have a feeling we aren't all going back alive."

"Maybe not," said Simon; "but I'll take my chance. I want to get my eyes on them silver mines. Every so often I've seen a pack train of silver come in from somewhere out here. I'd like to find out where they dig it."

"I do not like to go back," said Menard, "once I have start' somewhere."

"Come on," said Simon, "it's getting light. We better move."

"What bothers me," said Dan, watching the horizon, "is it *too* plain. If these Camanches are so slippery, they can do better than that."

"I'm sure Toroblanco knows what he do," said Menard. "He's prob'ly have scouts out behind to see if they are followed, and I will bet you a thousand sous right now he knows we're here and he can tell the colour, age, and sex of every mule we've got."

The trail followed the Big Wichita. With women and children, Dan had figured, they wouldn't travel very fast, and he would have to look sharp to keep from running into them. But Toroblanco's Kotsotekas were making tracks. They cut south-west to hit the upper waters of the Brazos, and Dan was disappointed to find it loaded with salt.

"Watch the mules," Dan warned. "They drink too much of that stuff, we'll be afoot."

They went west to the Salt Plains. Here the country was level and dry but cut by deep *arroyades*. The grass grew poor and scanty, and only occasionally did they find a spring of sweet water. The springs were seldom big enough to make a stream, for the water soaked into the sand as fast as it flowed.

Dan looked back towards the east. There was nothing but flat plains behind them. "We've come four days."

"We must be gettin' close to the Yarner," said Simon.

"What's the Yarner?"

"The Staked Plains. You come to a big cliff that goes hundreds of miles north and south, and up on top is all level prairie, no water, no wood. If there's any water

131

holes, nobody knows them but the Camanches and the Cayugas."

"It isn't too late to go back," said Dan.

Simon tossed a bone into the ashes of the fire. "Keep your eyes this way," he said in a conversational tone, "but behind you, maybe half a mile, is an Indian watching."

Dan went on eating as if he had not heard. Menard paused for only an instant. "How many?" asked Dan.

"I count eight," Simon said presently.

Dan got up and walked casually over to his saddle-bag. He got a carrot of tobacco and bit off a chew. He put the tobacco back in the saddle-bag and returned to his former place around the dead fire. "I see them. It looks like feathers sticking up over the grass. Seems mighty careless."

Simon looked troubled. "Maybe Poeyfarré was right. Maybe I shouldn't of come on this sashay, but it's too late to go back," he added hastily.

"How can they sneak up on us on a flat prairie?" Dan asked.

"With Camanches," said Simon, "you don't wonder how. If a Camanche put his mind to it, he could steal your moccasins off your feet without waking you up. Only," he added, "they don't go around stealing moccasins."

"I would say," said Dan, "the best thing for us is to stay in open country. That way we have a chance to watch them."

Menard wiped his greasy fingers on his buckskin pants. He looked towards Dan, but his eyes were on the prairie beyond Dan's shoulder. Then he laughed. "Camanches! You are get' nervous, *amigo*. Those are not Camanches, my frien', those are *cabreu* — goats."

Simon let out a sigh of relief. "Antelope," he said. "I should of known. Those horns, curved on the end, look like Indians' feathers from a distance."

"So now you quit worry," said Menard.

Dan felt the heavy weight of possible tragedy to one of them if not all. "We would have time to go back," he said quietly. "The Camanches cannot outrun us if we light out across the plains. It is only that we have to be so careful that they are staying ahead of us."

"Nope." Simon was positive. "I started. I'll finish, if I do lose my hair."

Menard eyed him soberly. "Losing your scalp, my frien', is the best thing that might happen to you in Camanche country."

The trail of the Camanche camp moved more to the south-west. The land became drier, grass scantier, game scarce, and the water almost undrinkable. Even the running water in the few small streams was as salty as sea water. Occasionally, following the Camanches' trail, they reached a buffalo wallow with a few inches of dirty, yellow-stained water. The mules drank this, and so did the men. "Is no time to be fussy," Menard observed.

"I'm not so sure," said Dan worriedly, "but what we need is something to head us the other way."

The hot winds struck them from the south and south-west — winds that shrivelled the sparse grass, that seemed to turn man and beast inside out and hold him up to the sun. The brackish water and the all-meat diet gave them diarrhœa. They found a cottonwood tree at a water hole, and Menard took the inside bark, boiled it and made a tea, which he told them to drink.

"Tastes like hell," said Simon. "It's more puckery than persimmons and more bitter than chinaberries."

"It cure you, though." And Menard was right.

Water became more of a problem. Two days later their mouths and throats were like leather. Menard got down from his horse, cut off the thick leaf of a prickly pear and peeled it with his knife. He gave them each a piece of the white meat. "Hold it in your mouth," he said. "It is better than a bullet or a piece of copper to draw water."

The hot winds beat down at them, making it hard to breathe. The water holes became mere buffalo tracks with a few spoonfuls of water. And they knew now that the Camanches were all around them, for Menard went half a mile back to their camp one morning, looking for a lost carrot of tobacco, and found a small piece of buckskin with some beadwork on it. "It wasn't there when we left this morning," he said. "It was dropped later."

Dan looked at the sun. "They are watching us, then."

Simon said, "It means we don't dare to turn back now. The Indians are always worst when you are on the run."

They reached another encampment of Toroblanco's band that evening, and Dan went out around the site of the camp and studied the ground. "They are only one day ahead," he announced when he came back.

"They're not eating reg'lar, either," Simon pointed out. "Look at the bones — turtles, lizards, horny toads, and snakes. Grub is gittin' scarce."

Menard scowled at the west. "We getting near the Caprock," he said. "I wondair if Toroblanco is going up there, or will he go north?"

"It couldn't be much worse up there," said Dan.

"Is worse," Menard said emphatically. "No water, more hot wind. Nothing to eat but the goats — and they are verr' difficult to kill on the high plains, for there is nothing to hide behind. Even the grass is too short this summer to hide a rattlesnake."

They camped back away from a water hole that night.

"Not close," Menard insisted.

His knowledge of the Salt Plains proved itself. During the night Dan was awakened by trampling hooves and the growl of a panther. He sat upright in his blanket and saw in the moonlight, down at the water hole, a big cat fastened around the neck of a deer. He shot without thinking. The panther screamed and fell to the ground. The deer sprang away into the darkness.

They dressed out the panther and went down in a hollow to build a fire. They sat up the rest of the night, eating every edible part of the panther, including its intestines.

When daylight came, Dan looked at their gaunt, unshaved faces. "I never realised how close we were to starving," he said.

"First time I been full in two weeks," said Simon.

Menard filled his pipe with his last scrap of tobacco. "That deer might still be around," he said wisely. "It weel not get too far from the water."

Simon picked up his rifle. "I'll saunter down to the mudhole and have a look."

"Watch where you're going," said Dan.

"That's my best trick," Simon assured him.

Menard scowled as Simon walked away. "Is dividing us up. I do not like."

Almost at the same time Dan heard the splat of small hooves in the mud. An antlered deer jumped from behind a mesquite bush and bounded away over the prairie, to disappear in the north-west.

Simon was near the hobbled mules. He caught his own, jerked off the rawhide link, stuffed it in his shirt, leaped on the mule bareback, and went off after the deer.

Menard and Dan caught the mules and saddled them. Dan kept watching the horizon where Simon had disappeared. They left Simon's saddle and his *alforjas* in a clump of beargrass. "He might come back looking for them," he said.

CHAPTER
FOURTEEN

They came to the next *arroyada*, a dry gash in the alkali earth whose whiteness glistened under the brilliant sun.

"Will be a hot day," said Menard.

The sun was now edging over the eastern horizon like a blazing arc of hot brass.

"There's a mudhole." Dan pointed. "That would be where the deer went."

"And here" — Menard got down — "is where Simon approach' the edge to get a shot."

"But he didn't shoot."

"No. We would hear a shot many miles this morning."

"Then he must be down there somewhere."

"The mule stood back here." Menard indicated droppings. "And then . . ."

Dan was down, holding the mule's reins. "All of a sudden," he said, "the mule took off at a gallop. It was scared."

"Scar' of what, I wonder. No panther would be so close, up here on the priarie, or Simon would have seen it."

Dan said harshly, "I'm afraid I know the answer to that."

"I'm listen."

"What if there were a couple of Camanches down in that *arroyada*, watching us? They'd hear him come up, and hide back against the bank. Then they'd find a way out, and come up behind him. That's what scared the mule. Mules don't like Indians anyway."

Menard nodded, his eyes narrow.

"The mule snorts and runs. Simon looks around. The Indians are flat on the ground. Simon starts after the mule, and an arrow . . ."

"An arrow can be merciful," said Menard.

Dan flinched. "There's no sign of blood. It wasn't an arrow. Anyway, he would have hollered."

Menard said, "We can trail him."

"They would leave one in the *cañon* to watch the ponies," Dan said thoughtfully, "while one or two of them went after him. While he was chasing the mule, they might have run after him and caught him before he could fire a shot."

"I theenk that is it."

"Then," Dan said grimly, "we've got to find him before they start to work on him."

Menard was watching the ground. "Here the ponies were brought up from the *cañon*."

Dan nodded. "Three ponies and a mule. Makes a plain trail."

They followed the trail at a trot. "It's uncanny," said Dan. "Four animals and four men disappeared off the face of the earth. There's nowhere to hide."

"There are plenty more *cañons*. They have gone into one and are following it, but not the way we might expect."

"We can tell when the trail goes down."

It turned to the left almost immediately, and they found themselves in a shallow draw. A man walking alongside his horse might be invisible from the prairie. They followed the tracks to the bottom of the draw, and came out in a small *cañon* with white alkali dirt sides. A stream ran through the bottom of it.

They rode, one on each side of the stream, watching for the exit of horses' tracks. They followed the stream for two miles, with the water diminishing in volume until finally it sank into the sand and flowed no farther.

"There are no tracks," said Menard. "Then we must go the other way."

Dan began to feel unexpected urgency. "We'd better hurry."

"We can cut across," said Menard. "We have been curving to the north."

"It'll save time . . . and time's getting short."

They rode out of the *arroyada* and came up on the plains again. The hot wind was now smothering, and beginning to pick up dust. "If we cut straight across this way," Dan said anxiously, "we should be able to gain on them."

They bore to the left, but the sun was high and the wind was stronger, and tiny particles of gravel began to beat against their hands and faces.

By now the sun was obscured, the dust having risen a considerable distance above the earth, and they could not be sure of directions. But Dan felt better when the mules stopped at the edge of an *arroyada*.

They found a way down in. There was a tiny stream in the bottom of this one, too, so they followed it up until they reached a place where it seeped out from the base of a high cliff. They examined the ground, and finally Dan shook his head. "If they came this way, they left the *cañon* before they got up here."

"We follow it down," said Menard. "They have to come out somewhere."

They stayed in the *cañon* for a mile; then the water soaked into the sand and disappeared as before.

"Wait a minute," said Dan. "It isn't as long now as it was."

Menard looked at him thoughtfully. He got down and tasted the water. When he arose he said sadly, "Is not the same water, *mon ami*."

Dan was incredulous. "You sure?"

"The other water was salty; this is sweet. The mules will love it. But we have found another stream."

"Where's the one we were following?"

"Is the big question."

Dan barked, "You're lost!"

Menard got out his pipe. He had no more tobacco for it but he clamped it between his teeth, and said, "We're both *norteado*."

"It isn't possible. I've seen men lost in the forest but never on the plains like this. In the meantime the Camanches have got Simon."

Menard did not comment.

Impatience began to overcome Dan. "We can't just sit here. No telling what those red heathens are doing to him."

Menard's answer was grave. "That also is true. What do you suggest?"

Dan got hold of himself with an effort. "We don't dare split up. That's the first thing. And the second thing is to decide where to look. There's so much dirt in the air we can't tell which way is west."

"Maybe we best stay here until the storm goes down."

"We can't sit here for days while the damned Camanches are torturing Simon."

"Very well," said Menard. "You lead the way. I am with you."

"I've got a feeling it doesn't run east and west," said Dan. "To me it runs north, so we'll choose half-way between."

"Better fill the water bags," said Menard. "In this part of the country there may be no more streams. We cannot know."

They filled the vellum-like buffalo paunches and hung them on the saddle-horns. They gave the mules a last chance to drink up. Then they started into the wind.

Three days later their food gave out. The wind was still hot and grinding, all day and all night, never letting up. Their noses began to bleed without provocation. They used up their water but found a mudhole the second day.

"There have been Camanches here," said Menard.

"How do you know?"

"See the little round spots in the soft ground near the water? That's where the squaws get down on their knees to drink."

"And the warriors?"

"Always they do not trust anybody. They put their hands into the water and balance on their hands and toes. The water takes away the hand marks, and they brush away the toe marks in the dry ground. But the squaws drink from their knees. Poeyfarré says that is Camanche custom." Menard turned his back to the wind. "Is hard to tell. The pony sign is hard, and the wind has blown away the trail or covered it up."

The next day the force of the wind abated, but the air was still filled with dirt. They found an *arroyada* that was truly an *arroyada*, for it was dry. Their water bags were empty, and the mules were braying piteously.

"There is a way, perhap', to find watair," said Menard. "Poeyfarré have told me."

They followed up the *arroyada* until they came to a ten-foot-high bank on the windward side. "Dig close to the bank," said Menard.

They dug up the soft sand until they had a hole knee-deep. The sand was moist, but there was no water.

"Wait a little while," said Menard. "Water will come."

And after Menard's "little while" there was water in the hole six inches deep. They drank and filled the bags, and let the hole fill again and again. Their only food now was parched corn and a pair of mud-dauber swallows that they killed with a stick. They ate the birds raw, while the mules foraged on the almost non-existent grass.

They started out the next morning, leather-lipped, cotton-mouthed. By afternoon they were walking, leading the mules. The wind died down completely that afternoon, and the sun became visible as it set, a great reddish-yellow omen.

Dan stared at it. "You know what that means? We're going west!"

But Menard shook his head. "Now, yes, but not for the last several days."

"How could that be?"

"We have make a big circle, and now we're going west all right, but we're back towards the Brazos."

"If we're that far east, we ought to be near water."

"The wind blows the water out of the ground. You can tell by watching the mules. They can smell water a long way, but they have not lifted their ears for two days."

They rested a while and started moving again after midnight. "The mules won't last long if we don't find water," said Dan.

"They will go a long time if you don't feed them."

Dan looked at Menard's blackened face, his cracked lips, his shrunken skin. "None of us are going much longer," he said.

Menard's eyes narrowed. "Two mules . . . two more days, maybe three."

They killed one of the mules that night and drank its blood, thick and purple. It gagged them, and it was salty, but it seemed to go into the dried-up tissues of their bodies. They cut off a ham and skinned it and ate it raw. Dan used the dirt to clean blood from his hands. "It's a shame the other mule can't eat meat," he said.

Menard shook his head. "That pile of skin and bones has not much longer to live."

They killed the second mule at the middle of the next day. They had crossed breaks in the earth, but there was no water in any of them, and Menard insisted that the wind had sucked it up. They ate a part of the second mule, and Menard got out his pipe and chewed on the stem. "Our last night unless we have some luck." His voice was hoarse.

"Do we still head west?"

"Good as any, since we don't know where we are. Tejas," he said, "is a mighty big place."

They took enough meat from the mule's carcass to carry them through the second day, and staggered on west. The sun was bigger, it seemed to Dan, and more scorching than any previous day. It sapped the moisture out of his skin and out of his flesh, and pretty soon he knew it would begin to dry out his bones, and that would be all.

Finally, in mid-afternoon, Menard sat down with his back against a clump of beargrass. His voice was a croak. "I'm through, *mon ami*. Give my love to the girls in Santa Fé."

Dan, standing, looked down at him. There was nothing left of Menard but skin and bone; his face was blackened; his lips were turned inside out and dry like old leather. "You stay here," Dan said. "I'm going to have a look. That beargrass seems familiar to me."

"Every clump of beargrass is like every other. They are not like women. Women are all different, but beargrass . . ." He fell over on his back.

Dan pulled him off the sharp spines at the ends of the long leaves. He noted the slackness in Menard's clothes, and shook his head.

He took his bearings, remembering the beargrass he had seen that day — now almost two weeks ago. He was still carrying his *alforjas*, and now he slung them over the beargrass so he would be sure to see the place. Then he went south-west.

He reached the edge of an *arroyada* and stood looking down at it, not realising at first what he was seeing. Then his eyes opened wide and he let out a croak. He ran back to Menard and dragged him up by the front of his shirt. "Come on, you Frenchie, there's water down there!"

"Water," said Menard, "is all alike, but women are all different."

Dan dragged him over the prairie to the *arroyada*. He found a place where they could get down. He laid Menard in the sand with his hands and wrists in the water, while he himself took a mouthful, careful at first not to swallow it. He washed his arms in it. He took off his clothes and lay in it, and his body seemed to soak it up like a sponge. Menard opened his eyes. The water on his hands seemed to revive him, and presently he, too, was rolling in the stream. Not until an hour later did they dare to take water into their stomachs, and finally Dan sat down and pulled on his clothes. "We're back where we started," he said. "If Simon hadn't gone for that deer, we'd be together yet."

"Is sad about Simon," said Menard. "But we have to find something to eat for ourselves."

"I'll get my rifle and we'll go up to the spring and wait. There was a chinaberry tree. Maybe another deer will come along."

"You damn' Englishman." Menard smiled. "You never quit going, do you?"

"Not while I can move. You going to walk, or you want me to carry you?"

"You get the rifle," Menard said, and Dan knew he was nearly gone in spite of the water. "I'll walk up the cañon and meet you." He looked at the fifteen-foot banks. "I could not climb those now."

Dan nodded. He made his way up a white-dirt draw and came out on the prairie. He saw the saddle-bags and went to them. He was so intent on getting the rifle that he didn't notice anything wrong until a swarthy man stood up just beyond the beargrass and said, "*Bienvenida*, Señor Shank', *mi amigo francés*."

Dan stared at Lieutenant Borica. The lieutenant had a big pistol in one hand.

"We have wait' around here several days for you, señor."

Dan looked at his rifle, half-standing in the beargrass, and swore.

"Back, if you please. Don't do anything foolish. My men are most unhappy with this abominable dust

146

storm and the hot sun which you have caused them to endure."

"What made you think we'd come back here?"

"First, I knew you couldn't cross the Llano Estacado, and it seemed reasonable that you would return by the same route you used in going out. Then the storm came up, and I knew you would be lost and would probably circle, so we waited here where there was water." He smiled sardonically. "Water is important out here."

"I heard," said Dan harshly.

"Where are your *compañeros?*"

"One is out yonder somewhere. The Camanches got him."

The lieutenant clucked sympathetically. "*Está malo.* And the other?"

Dan looked at the rifle again, but Borica had moved in front of it. For a second he debated, but the answer was inescapable. Even if Menard escaped the Spaniards, he had to have food or he wouldn't last the next day. Dan took a deep breath. "Down there," he said.

Borica motioned, and two Spanish soldiers got up from where they had been lying on the ground beyond the beargrass. They ran down into the *arroyada.*

"What's the charge this time?" asked Dan. "We aren't violating any laws."

"You will please turn around. That's fine. *Gracias.* You will see I have respect for your resourcefulness. You damned Englishmen are likely to try anything."

Dan turned around and walked slowly towards the *arroyada*. The other six soldiers were at the bottom of it. They had not been over half a mile from where Dan and Menard had found water. Dan went down a water-gashed draw, followed by Borica, who had brought his rifle.

The two soldiers now came down the stream with Menard. He looked at Dan and smiled weakly. "It looks like they have us now, *mon ami*."

"They've got us," said Dan. "But what for?"

"It is a pleasure to do one's duty without a thousand Indians waiting to shoot one in the back," observed Borica. "You will observe the tables are turned, and I am now able to obey the orders of His Most Catholic Majesty without interference. I arrest you for being without passports, without trading licences, and for smuggling rifles to the Indians in defiance of the laws of the Indies."

Dan stared at him. "You must be *loco*! I've only got that one rifle, and I had that back at the Wichita village. I've still got it. You can't accuse me of selling rifles to the Indians."

"It is worth inquiring why you risked your lives to come into Camanche country if you did not wish to sell rifles to the Indians."

Dan hesitated. "We were looking for silver mines," he said finally.

"What would you do with silver if you found it?"

"Take it to Nacogdoches or Béxar, of course."

"That I find very difficult to believe," said Borica, "in the face of the evidence which you left behind at this camp."

148

"What kind of evidence?"

"You will be duly advised when you get to Béxar."

"Wait a minute. Simon Jeffreys — he's out there. The Camanches got him."

The lieutenant smiled ironically. "By this time," he assured Dan, "you have nothing to worry about on his account. Ortiz!"

"Sí, señor."

"See these men are fed. It is a shame to waste food on such criminals, but the inspector has ordered that all arrested men be taken to Béxar."

Dan kept still. The lingering last words of Borica's statement warned him that not a very sharp line separated him from death even now.

He looked at the west and bowed his head for a moment. Then he said to Borica, "When do we start?"

"In the morning."

CHAPTER
FIFTEEN

Dan awoke before daylight, with a Spanish toe in his ribs and a gnawing hunger in his stomach. "*¡Arriba!*" was the command. "Up! Get some food in your belly. It's a long way to go to-day."

Dan got up, grumbling, and went to the fire where a Spanish soldier in long moustaches was stirring a savoury-smelling stew in a big kettle.

"Which way are we going to-day?"

"Due south to the Tork-an-ho-no, which we should strike at the Montes Dobles — Double Mountains. It will be an easy day's ride across the Salt Plains."

The Spaniards did not get under way very fast. It was mid-forenoon before the stew was ready, and they took their time eating, squatting around the kettle, and *platicando* — indulging in small talk.

Dan had time to learn how to wrap a thin *tortilla* around his forefinger and use it as a spoon to dip up the stew, eating *tortilla* and all each time.

"It is good," said Borica, "that you become familiar with our customs."

"Especially," said Menard through a mouthful of stew, "since we are likely to see the inside of a Spanish *juzgado* for the next five years."

To all this Dan listened carefully. Some of Borica's phrases he was to hear many times more, he knew instinctively.

"Will there be a judge at Béxar to hear our case?" he asked.

"*Seguro.* There is a judge in Béxar every year, *señor.* Your case will be heard promptly, as soon as the judge arrives."

"From what I've heard," said Menard, "promptly in the Spanish language doesn't mean the same as it does in English."

Borica said blandly, "Those things are no more pressing than when you entered New Spain without a passport or a trading licence."

They had trouble getting their mules together. One had broken his hobbles and strayed too far for recovery, and another had apparently been bitten by a snake, for his front leg was badly swollen and the mule was down.

The corporal told Borica about it. The lieutenant went to look at the mule, and ended by shooting him in the head. "I don't like to waste powder and lead on a mule," he said while he was reloading the pistol, "but he might recover, and the Camanches would capture him. We are under strict orders not to let horses or mules fall into the hands of the Indians, for they would trade them for rifles."

"And you can't give them rifles because they would use them against the Spanish?"

"*Sí.*"

Dan said, "Hmph!" but Borica chose to ignore it. His mule was brought up, and Borica mounted. It was

151

astonishing, Dan noted, how the man changed when he was horseback. His whole figure assumed a regal bearing unlike that of Borica on foot. He had had a somewhat overbearing manner on the ground, and now he still had it, but on the ground it had seemed an unpleasant extension of his power as an officer, while on horseback or muleback he seemed to have a right to it.

"I regret to say," Borica told them, "that with the loss of our two extra mules you will be forced to walk."

Dan looked out at the white plains with the heat waves shimmering above them. "You don't expect us to keep up with a mule, do you?"

"I might be forgiven if I did," said Borica. "You English and French are so proud of your abilities. But, no, I hardly expect that. If you make six or seven leagues a day, it will be sufficient for our purpose."

"Six or seven leagues — twenty miles!"

"I trust you will not force me to anything unpleasant, señor."

"I'm sure," said Dan, "you could be no more unpleasant at my forcing than you are by nature."

They started off across the dazzling plain. The sun was high and hot. There was no wind.

"Couldn't you send a detachment to look for Simon?" asked Dan.

"You would have me jeopardise my command for one man — one Englishman. No, I don't think *el señor inspector* would approve that."

"The Camanches . . ."

152

"I have said already, the Indians waste no food on a man they intend to kill. They have no prisons. Either they make a slave of a captive or they torture him. At any rate, I am sure your friend is a long way from here, and we do not know which way to go to look for him."

They made a dry camp that evening on the plains. There was no water and no wood; not even the ubiquitous mesquite or cottonwood. The soldiers gathered buffalo chips for fuel while Dan and Menard, tired from a day's marching and exhausted by the heat and lack of water, lay on their backs to rest.

That night was hot. The fire died out, and the *coyotl* sang around them. In spite of his weariness, Dan found it hard to sleep. He lay on a quilt, watching the brilliant stars, wondering where Simon was that night. And twice, sometime after midnight, he heard a killdeer cry.

Menard heard it too. "That bird never sits in a bush or a tree — always on the ground."

"Something disturbed it," Dan said in a low voice.

They listened for a moment.

Dan whispered, "There's something out there."

"Maybe," said Menard. "Whatever it is, we would be fools to go looking in the dark."

Dan rolled back. "They wouldn't let us, anyway."

Presently Menard whispered, "There may be an attack by the Camanches at dawn. Do you have any weapon?"

"No, they took my rifle and all."

He felt the flat, cold steel of a knife blade on his arm. "Keep this. I stole two of them from the *cocinero* — the cook. Keep it out of sight, and don't use it for anything unless the Indians attack us."

Dan took the knife and slid it under his belt, inside his shirt.

"See that it is at your back when they search you, for they will pat your stomach."

"All right."

He went to sleep finally, but it was an uneasy sleep, filled with bad dreams and frequent awakenings. He looked at Menard, who was sleeping soundly with his head bent down a little, at the guard who paced back and forth along the mules, with a rifle over one shoulder, at the inscrutable darkness that hid whatever was out there.

He understood a little better now why the Tejas country was so inimical to man, for it was enormous and it was hostile in many different ways — from heat, from aridity, from scarcity of wood and absence of food, from wind and dust, and probably from cold in the winter, from many tribes of savage Indians, from incredible distances and the ever-present alkali that coloured the ground as if salt water had flooded it for many years.

He stayed awake for a long time after that, listening for strange sounds, hearing little but the *coyotl*, for up here on the dry land there were few insect noises. Occasionally, with his ear to the ground, he could hear a sound of digging, and concluded it was a badger going into a prairie-dog hole.

Finally he slept a little more, uneasily, until he heard the *cocinero* get up and build his fire.

154

He thought they would be under way in a hurry that day, but it was not so. The Spaniards took their time, and again it was well into the morning before they got strung out, Dan and Menard both walking in the heavy white dust kicked up by the mules.

They had been on the move for two hours when Menard pointed at the sky ahead. "*Zopilotes* — turkey buzzards," he said.

Borica saw them at about the same time. He pulled up his mule and stopped the column. Dan managed to walk alongside him. "It may be a trap," said Borica. "The buzzards being so high in the air would indicate the animal is still alive. That is unusual itself, out on the plains. Generally an injured animal does not live long."

"It might be a stray buffalo bull," said Menard.

"Out here it would be killed by the wolves in a very short time."

Dan frowned. "D'you suppose — ?"

Borica looked down at him. "It could be your friend. It is a favourite trick of the Camanches to find out which way a party is going and then to stake out a victim where he will be found."

Dan swallowed. "Simon . . ."

Borica sighed. "I suppose we shall have to see. The king's business can wait. You'd better come."

Dan nodded.

"Ortiz! Bosque! *Abajo!*"

Two Spaniards dismounted and turned their mules over to Dan and Menard.

"Santos! Manzanares!"

Two Spaniards fell in behind. The lieutenant went forward at a trot, standing in his stirrups, his big rowels jingling. Dan and Menard spread out a little, staying behind him but not clouded by the white dust his mule raised.

They covered a mile. Then suddenly Borica drew up his mule. "*¡Allá!*" he said.

It was something very low on the ground. The buzzards were volplaning high above; half a dozen *coyotes* sat up on their haunches, just out of rifle range.

"Is that what you hunt, *amigo*?" asked Borica.

Dan stared at the ground. Buried up to his neck, but still alive, was Simon Jeffreys. At least, he sounded alive, for hoarse croaks came from his leathery throat.

Dan slid down from the mule. With the blazing sun high overhead, he didn't know whether Simon saw them or not, for, though Simon's head was turned towards them, his eyes showed little recognition. It might have been that he was blinded by the sun, for his eyelids had been removed. Nor was that all. He had been scalped. His head was oozing blood, and a great cloud of blowflies arose from him as Dan ran up.

Dan began to dig with his knife. He didn't know whether Simon recognised him or not. Only those odd croakings continued.

Feverishly Dan threw dirt to one side while Menard dug on the other. They dug his arms free, while Borica watched silently. They they got him by the arms, and to Dan's surprise, his body came up.

Dan looked up at Borica. "We need help!" he shouted.

156

Borica shook his head slowly. "There is nothing in this world we can do for him."

"We'll make a litter between two mules," said Dan.

"I do not think he would want to live," Borica said.

"It doesn't make any difference what you think," Dan snapped. "We'll keep him alive as long as we can."

"There is no water," said Borica. "A shot in the back of the head would be quicker and easier."

"He's still alive!" shouted Dan.

Borica nodded. "Santos!"

They used a blanket stretched between two mules. Dan waved off the flies, but the hot sun was impossible to guard against. Simon had grown quiet, and his face was white. Only the croakings still came from the leathery throat.

"He's trying to say something," said Menard. "I can't hear what it is."

"I think I know," said Borica. He took out his pistol and thrust it, butt-first, into Simon's hand. Dan frowned.

A change came over Simon's mutilated face. It was almost as if something pleased him. Then he put the muzzle of the pistol between his teeth and pulled the trigger.

Borica reloaded the pistol calmly. "I will give you an hour to bury him," he said, "though he's an infidel."

Dan and Menard went to work. They made the grave as deep as they could. When Borica announced the time was up, they laid the body in the bottom of the hole and covered it with the whitish dirt.

"Is too bad. There are not even rocks to cover him," said Borica.

"You think the *coyotls* will dig him up?"

Borica looked towards the horizon. In all quarters, sitting on their haunches out of rifle range, were prairie wolves — probably twenty in all.

"It has been a dry summer," said Borica. "They will dig deep."

"I'd like to stay here and beat their brains out!" said Dan, suddenly losing control.

"It would do you no good. Besides, it cannot be permitted; you are a prisoner. It is not the fault of the *coyotls* anyway. Besides, they will pay, for next year there will be few rabbits and fewer *coyotls*. Now, señores, if you will geev me those knives . . ."

CHAPTER
SIXTEEN

They reached the Tock-an-ho-no that night, and the next day went around the Double Mountains and kept due south through a wide strip of mesquite, prickly pear, and post oak.

Dan and Menard were heavy-hearted as they walked in the dust, and even the Spaniards did not seem as talkative as they had been. The train came out on rolling tablelands heavy with grama grass and mesquite grass, and the mules began to graze voraciously.

"I have sorrow for your friend," Borica told them the first evening they camped on the Pash-a-he-no fork of the Río Colorado. "Perhaps you know now why we do not give rifles to the accursed Camanches."

"If that's a sample, I understand it," said Dan harshly.

"And still you must remember the Camanche is only doing what he has been taught to do. He doesn't want us in his country, and he takes this means of warning us to stay away."

"When they turn me loose at Béxar I'm coming back," Dan said grimly, "and I'll massacre every Camanche in New Spain."

Borica dipped up a *tortilla* full of the eternal stew.

"Is a fine ambition," he observed, "but I theenk your anger will be cooled by the time you are released from Béxar."

"Maybe." But Dan remembered the way the Camanches had left Simon back there on the Salt Plains, and he still felt like fighting somebody over it . . .

Béxar was a town of adobes, large and small, clustered along the Río San Antonio, and practically every street was a canal through which water flowed and in which men, women, and children splashed, dived, and paddled, all without any sort of clothing and all apparently without thought of their nakedness.

It was a warm afternoon when they rode through the narrow streets. The buildings were all one story high and with few windows, but the streets were fairly straight and regular. They passed a whitewashed church with a large belfry, and all the time they were assailed by barking dogs, trying to dodge squawking chickens and bleating goats, and at the same time running a constant gauntlet of curious black eyes — for everybody, male and female, clothed and unclothed, stared at them, and cries of "*¡Los ingleses! ¡Los ingleses!*" ran through the town and up and down the narrow streets and across the *acequias* with their shallow waters.

They were taken to an unusually large building and led inside, where it was cool and dark. Borica turned them over to a grizzled Spaniard who took them to a lower floor, pushed them into a cell, and clanged shut an iron door. Dan heard the lock screech as the big key turned in it. Then the grizzled jailer's footsteps faded away on the dirt floor, and they were alone. Suddenly the sounds and the brightness of the sunshine and splashing of the waters were shut out, and it was as if they were in a different world.

But presently they could see, for a narrow slot above their heads admitted air and light.

Dan looked around. "They must have been short on furniture when they built this *juzgado*."

Menard sat in a corner. "At least it's out of the sun, and away from the Camanches, and I suppose we'll be fed."

"I didn't ask him about getting out."

"Don' waste your time," said Menard. "We may be here for years."

"Years!"

"The Spanish don't believe in hurry. The only time they get excited is at a bullfight."

"Do you think we'll have blankets?"

"Probably not. They expect us to buy them."

"We're not supposed to have any money."

"But they know we have it anyway," Menard said imperturbably. "They expect us to buy food and knives and pay for our own washing."

"It's a strange kind of prison."

Menard lay on his back, with one arm under his head, sucking his pipe. "It's not bad, as prisons go. I'll be able to get some tobacco now."

Dan paced the hard dirt floor for a while. "I can't stay in here," he said. "I've got a lot of things to do."

An hour later a soft whisper came from the iron bars that formed the door. "*Señores . . . ingleses.*"

Dan went to the door, while Menard lay where he was, smiling. "Yes," said Dan.

A girl in a red and yellow skirt, white, loose-fitting blouse, and jet black hair looked up at him. "*Señor, qué alto!* — How tall you are!"

"Your first friend," said Menard.

"What do you want?" asked Dan.

"I have something for you, *señor* — bread, soap, melons. What you want?"

"We can't buy," said Dan. "We're prisoners." It was in his mind that she had been sent as a spy to see if they had money.

"You do not have to buy," she said in that strange, soft, clipped accent. "Is for you — a gift."

"No, we can't —"

"You better let me take charge," said Menard. "The greatest insult you can offer a Spanish woman is to turn down a gift of food."

Dan looked at the girl again. She was holding a bundle through the bars. He took it; her hands were very white and smooth.

"*Gracias,*" he said finally.

"*No hay nada.*" She smiled and glided away as gracefully as a leaf in a warm breeze.

Menard said lazily, "If you look under the cornbread, you will no doubt find money."

Dan sat down and opened the square of linen cloth on his lap. He handed the hard, dry cones of bread to

162

Menard. "Well, strike me down! You're right! Two big silver reales! How did you know about this?"

"Poeyfarré," Menard said complacently. "I wish you had reminded her to bring some tobacco."

But tobacco came within another half-hour, in the form of a bundle of corn-shuck cigarros and some live coals in a small brass bucket. They thanked the second girl, who seemed reluctant to leave.

"If we can get enough money to bribe the jailer," said Menard, "the girls will stay all night."

"Not for me," said Dan.

Menard, smoking a cigarro, turned on his side. "Are you still thinking of that woman in Baltimore?"

"Maybe."

Menard turned on his back. "She's not worth it. Simon told me about her."

"I asked her to marry me."

"You were one damn' fool for asking her in the first place, and you are one damn' fool for remembering it in the second place. What's the matter with these girls?"

The dirt floor was hard to sleep on. "Dirt is harder than stone," Menard said, "when it's packed down by bare feet for a few hundred years."

The next day the jailer appeared with a small pot of *guisado* — a thick stew with a few pieces of rank-tasting goat meat — and a pile of *tortillas*.

"When do we get out of here?" Dan asked.

The grizzled old man shrugged. "Is not me — the courts. I do not know. Maybe the judge come from Méjico City next month, next year. *¿Quién sabe?*"

163

"What's your name?" asked Dan.

"No . . ."

"*¿Cómo sé llama?*"

"Pablo Serrano."

"Well, look, Don Pablo, here's a silver peso. Can you tell me what the evidence is against us?"

Pablo took the coin. "I theenk so, but may cost money, more than this, *señor*." He put the money in a pocket in his skin-tight trousers and went out noiselessly on the dirt floor.

"To-morrow," Menard predicted, "he'll be back for more money."

They ate well that afternoon and evening, with a constant stream of white-bloused visitors who brought more to eat than two men could ordinarily handle, but they had been a long time on the plains and ate voraciously — fruit, bread, tamales — and drank wine.

"You never had such a fine life in Pennsylvania," said Menard. "We have taken in three more pesos to-night."

"I can't understand it," said Dan. "Why do they want to give us things?"

"Is a long story," said Menard, sipping his wine. "Is their way of rebelling against their husbands. In Spain the man is absolute master. He goes where and when he pleases. He does what he pleases. He has mistresses and concubines. The Spanish women hate them for it, but there is nothing they can do, except take lovers."

"How . . ."

"Symbolism, perhaps. In making gifts to you and me, a Spanish woman is expressing her resentment of centuries of domination and cruelty. Unfaithfulness to her husband, either in body or in mind, is her greatest satisfaction, for the Spanish men lack the vigour they once had. They get up late in the morning, they have chocolate, they ride, always leisurely, on their estates, they sit in the sun, *platicando*, always *platicando*, talking and dreaming of days when they were great conquerors and their galleons ruled the seven seas. So it is peculiarly fitting that the Spanish women hit back at their vanity in this way."

"You learned all that from Poeyfarré?"

"The theory," Menard said lazily, "I leave to Poeyfarré. The facts I have ascertain' for myself."

They had more visitors around supper time, with a pot of *frijoles*, *tortillas*, and *vino*, all brought by dusky-skinned, black-haired, graceful girls who wore lovely small shoes but never any stockings, and who stayed and talked in broken English and some Spanish until they were practically crowded out by others.

Dan said later, "It's a strange kind of jail where you can have all the visitors you want and they can bring you anything."

"New Spain is a land of contradictions. To-day you live in prison like a king; to-morrow you may be riding a burro across the desert of the Bolsón de Mapimí with your feet shackled under his belly. It is best to take things as they come, to enjoy them when you may. It is not desirable to question one's good fortune. What more can you ask?"

165

That night old Pablo came down with a candle in a square lantern. "I can tell you about the evidence, señor, but is very risky," he said. "*El señor capitán* is constantly watching."

Menard puffed on his pipe. "How dangerous, Pablo?"

"I shall have to bribe an orderly in the captain's office."

"How about a gold quadruple-piastre piece?" asked Dan.

The *carcelero's* eyes glittered in the dim candlelight. "Perhaps it can be arranged."

Dan handed him a small gold piece. "I want to know the facts," he warned.

"In the morning, señor, I shall tell you."

He padded off along the dirt hallway and they heard his soft footfalls go up the dirt stairsteps. They were in darkness except for the twinkle of the stars through the narrow slit of a window far above their heads. "The women brought candles this afternoon," Menard noted; "but we don't need them just yet unless you have some letter writing to do."

Dan thought of Sarah, but somehow writing Sarah from prison didn't seem fitting. He remembered his mother and sisters, but he didn't want to worry them. "It will keep," he said.

A whisper at the iron bars. A high-pitched voice, clear, musical in its quality. "Señores."

"¿Quién es?" asked Menard, not moving.

"Guadalupe."

"Are you the one who was here first?"

The answer was pathetic in its eagerness. "*Sí, señor.*"

"*Bienvenida,*" said Menard. "Isn't it late for you to be out?"

"My *mamá* thinks I am home asleep."

"*¿Qué novedades?* What is the news?"

"*No hay mucho.*" She paused. "I have a key from Don Pablo, if you wish to walk around outside."

"What did I tell you?" said Menard, getting up. "Unlock the door, *señorita.*" Dan heard the key in the huge old lock, the tumblers screeching as they moved. "I take it, *mon ami,* you are not interested in going walking with Lupe."

Dan frowned in the dark.

"*Bien,*" said Menard. "I must do my duty." He got up and went silently across the floor. The door swung open, and there was a moment or two when the two dark figures were close.

"Pablo may not like this."

"Pablo won' be down to-night, I guarantee."

Dan heard the thud of Menard's feet on the dirt steps, the tiny sound of the girl's slippers alongside. He went back and looked at the stars through the slit of a window.

Pablo was back at mid-afternoon with a *guisado* hot enough with chilli peppers to burn the lining of a man's throat. "I have at great cost found what is the evidence against you, *señores.*"

"Let's hear it."

"It has taken all the gold you gave me, and I —"

Dan tossed him another peso.

Pablo brightened. "It is that there are two rifles of English make which were found at your camp-site, señor."

Dan took a step forward. "Two English rifles? New or old?"

"But quite new. They still have the lard on them."

"And English?"

"So I am told, but that I do not see for myself. They are in a long box of wood, and I am allow' to see them but my old eyes cannot read the words."

"Where are these rifles?"

"In the captain's office, señor."

Dan paced the floor. "How can we get a look at those rifles?"

There was nothing sly about Pablo when he answered, "That is not easy."

"What's the difference?" Menard drawled. "They're rifles, aren't they?"

"It makes a difference to me where they came from."

"Not as long as you're in here."

"And who planted them on us," said Dan.

"That's not important either. The lieutenant probably found them somewhere and had to bring back somebody for trial. He found us in Camanche territory and so he figured we were the ones."

"Either that," Dan said suddenly, "or he was paid to bring us back, and the rifles were put where he could find them."

Menard sat up straighter. "You are getting verr' smart to this country, mon ami. You theenk that man from Natchitoches . . ."

"Poeyfarré wouldn't do it, would he?"

"Positive' not. Poeyfarré never did that to a man who has fight with him."

"Then it was Meservy. He put the rifles where they would throw guilt on us; then he told Borica where to look."

"Is maybe right. Borica started east, and the Spaniards do not like Camanche country."

"I've got to find out who made those rifles, and what year."

"Try my friend Lupe. She's a persuasive girl, and she asked about the *hombre alto*."

"When will she be back?"

"To-night, perhaps, and every night." Menard sighed. "I like women. They relieve the monotony of life. But they can be demanding too."

"I must know what is said on those rifles — the maker and the year of manufacture."

"That may not be easy," Menard told him. "Not too many of these Spaniards can read and write."

Dan himself walked along the glistening canals in the moonlight with Lupe that night. The radiant warmth of her body near his was soothing, but he kept his mind on the problem he had set out to solve.

"I do not know," she said in her bird-like whisper, looking up at him. "I weel have to bribe somebody to read them for me."

"I've got money."

"Money ees not necessary, *señor*. Eef you —"

He kissed her, and it was like throwing a lighted torch into his bloodstream. He got back to the jail feeling like a firecracker about to explode. He passed Pablo, snoring on a pallet on the floor, and went downstairs to the cell. The iron-barred door was open, and Menard was gone. By the time he got back, Dan was getting his pulse down to normal. "I thought maybe you had escaped," he told Menard.

Menard stretched. "Not from this *juzgado*. We'll never be in a better one."

He sat back in the corner, singing softly to himself, "*Ay, chinita que sí, ay, que dame tu amor —*"

"A guitar," said Dan, "is all you need."

"Don't worry, *mon ami*. To-morrow will bring a guitar. I have suggest' it."

The guitar came the next night, and so did Lupe, and Margarita, and Panchita, and half a dozen others. Life in the *juzgado* began to be less monotonous than Dan would have thought possible.

"And yet," Dan said one morning, "that doggoned Lupe hasn't found out about the rifles."

"Maybe Lupe has more sense than you have," Menard said easily. "Maybe she knows that when you find out about the rifles, the honeymoon will be over."

Dan studied him. "Maybe that's it."

"It isn't every day she finds *un hombre tan alto*."

"But . . ."

"And you are just fool enough to bust up a *ménage* like this because of whatever is on those rifles."

"What's on those rifles is a lot more important to a lot more people than what goes on in Béxar."

"That's the hell of it all," said Menard. "You English have such an abominable sense of duty."

So the months went along. Winter came, but in Béxar it was only a milder form of summer, and on the few cold days Dan and Menard had plenty of wool blankets and hot food to keep them warm. The next summer came, and it was cool in their cell during the daytime. At night they walked the dusty trails around the town, smelled the delicate fragrance of the mesquite blossoms, and bathed in the canals. Then again it was winter and again summer, and still no word from Méjico or Sevilla, and still no judge to hear their case.

With the financial assistance of Lupe and others, Dan had set up business as a cobbler, and was soon making a very good living selling handmade shoes. Then one day, while Dan was finishing up a pair of cowhide boots, there was a fluster among the *señoritas*, and Pablo Serrano stalked through.

"You weel come with me," he ordered.

They went. Pablo refused explanations. He locked the door on them.

An hour later a second Spaniard came in, carrying hammers, straps of iron, and a small forge and bellows. He fitted a band of iron around Menard's left leg and riveted it there with the hammer. He put another on the right leg.

Dan said to Menard, "You must have been out with Borica's girl-friend."

"You don' listen to the gossip," Menard said sadly. "Borica no has been here for many months."

Dan tried to question the blacksmith.

"*No savvy*," the smith said, his hammer ringing on the rivets. "*No hablo inglés*."

He put fifteen feet of heavy chain between the ankle collars and riveted those also.

"Well," said Menard, "you are winning no foot races for a while."

Pablo came back about dark.

"What are these chains for?" Dan asked. "We haven't done anything."

"No, señor." Pablo shook his head. "You have done notheeng, but you are inglés, aren't you?"

"Yes," Dan said cautiously.

"The English colonies in America have rebell' and are fighting against the King. There is a war."

"That's none of my doing."

Pablo left their olla on the floor and went out, locking the door. He turned back. "The Council of the Indies does not know which side to have sympathy. The British we hate, for they have destroy' our Great Armada. But also the colonies we fear. If this rebellion last a long time, it may spread to New Spain. There could be disastrous results for the Spanish colonies. Therefore we have orders to take no chances. You must both be kept in heavy irons. It is the word from the viceroy in Méjico."

Dan had no trouble in understanding. He had been well coached in the Spanish language by this time.

"How long does this last?"

"I do not know, señor. You will be taken to Chihuahua and thence to Méjico, to await a decision by His Most Catholic Majesty."

CHAPTER
SEVENTEEN

Three days later they left Béxar, still with the heavy chains fastened to their legs, riding on burros. Their way out of Béxar was lined with Spanish girls, some weeping, some laughing, all with presents of clothing, food, and money. The men were part of a pack train which was escorted by a *capitán* and twelve soldiers. They went south-west to Presidio del Norte, up the Rio Grande and across the mountain country to Paso. There they were joined by a wealthy *hacendado* and his *señora* who travelled in a stage coach. They went across the desert to Chihuahua, along a road littered with the remains of two-wheeled Mexican carts.

In Chihuahua their chains were knocked off and they were well fed. There the inhabitants used the black *punche* for tobacco, and the bare-legged Mexican women smoked as incessantly as the men.

There were huge, clumsy European coaches drawn by seven mules and filled with black-eyed women, but none as inviting as those dressed only in shoes, skirt, and blouse, who watched from doorways smoking their inevitable *cigarros* and murmuring softly, "*¡Probrecitos! ¡Probrecitos!*"

They were in Chihuahua six months and lived well, but Dan could find out nothing about the course of the rebellion except that the colonists were still fighting, and a Colonel Washington from Virginia had been put in command of the colonial forces.

They could easily have escaped, but there was nowhere to go except across the hundreds of miles of desert and mountains, and they would not have got far.

They went on to Durango, famed for the beauty of its women, and stayed two weeks. They might as well have been guests of the town, for they were allowed to go to *fandangos* and even *bailes*. Still they were showered with gifts, and a wealthy Mexican woman gave them two fine horses to continue their trip to the city of Méjico.

In Méjico they were driven into a courtyard that looked like a stable, with doors opening all around it. Big rusty gates clanged behind them, and presently heads appeared in doorways and finally a man walked out on the cobblestones.

"*¿Por qué son VV. aquí?*"

"We're prisoners," said Dan, squinting to get a better look at the man. It chilled him, for the man looked like a dried-up mummy with a purple skin.

Others came out, and Dan and Menard both shrank back, for they were covered with sores, some without noses or fingers or ears.

Menard was crossing himself.

"First time I knew you had religion," said Dan.

"It may be the last time. Do you know where we are?"

174

"In Méjico, as far as I know."

"In a lepers' hospital," said Menard.

Dan choked. "They don't expect us to live with them, do they?"

"I hope not so," Menard said fervently, "but this is Méjico."

Two soldiers came out presently and, without concern, escorted them to a dirt-floored room and locked them in with iron bars. A while later a blacksmith appeared and asked in Spanish, "How big you want the collars, eh?"

Dan looked at him. "Is that log-chain going on?"

"*Sí, señor.*" He had two pieces of chain, each about eight feet long. "You want them tight, eh?"

Dan showed the *herero* a silver peso and said, "Big enough so we can slip out of them when nobody is looking."

The *herrero* put the peso in his pocket and went to work. He finished his riveting and turned to Menard, who also had a peso ready. After the man left, Dan said, "I think I can get them over my feet."

"If you can't," said Menard, "you sure wasted a peso."

Dan observed, "There's no use wearing them unless the *capitán* comes around."

"He'll be around once a day. We'd better keep them on until we find out exactly what time he comes."

Captain Paredón did not come around until the next day, and there was a considerable hubbub preceding his arrival, so that Dan and Menard had no trouble getting their chains in place.

175

The captain was a tall man, dark complexioned and hawk-nosed. He glanced at the chains on their legs, at the blankets on the dirt floor, and the single door that was the only break in the stone walls. "You are being fed, *no*?"

Dan nodded.

"A few *clacos* will buy you a glass of *pulque* now and then. You should be very comfortable until a decision comes from the king."

Dan stood up. "Have you got those two rifles that we are supposed to have smuggled into Tejas?"

The captain's eyes narrowed. His right hand rested on the pistol in his holster. "We have them."

"Is there any other evidence against us?"

"Isn't that enough?"

"Not for me." Dan showed the officer a gold quadruple. "I want to know the maker of those rifles and the year they were made."

Paredón took the gold piece. "I will see what can be done." He left. Two soldiers closed the door and locked it with a huge brass padlock.

"That was wan quick way to spend four pesos," said Menard.

"I'll get my money's worth," said Dan, "and then some."

The blacksmith was in the next morning to inspect their leg irons. "*El capitán* comes every day after his siesta. The chains must be in place," he warned.

"They will be."

That afternoon Paredón came into their cell. He glanced at the irons, and held out a piece of paper to Dan. "You read, *señor*?"

"I read."

"This is what it says on the two rifles."

Dan took the paper. On it, in the broad strokes of a turkey-quill pen, were the words and figures: Wm. Watts 1772.

Dan hardened when he read it. He started to put the paper in his pocket.

"I am sorry, *señor*, I cannot give you the paper."

"I paid you for it," Dan said belligerently.

"You paid for the information. You do not need the paper. You know what it says."

"Yes."

Paredón crumpled the heavy piece and thrust it inside of his red-lined coat. "Then our bargain is *terminado*, no?"

"As far as it went," said Dan. "But there's another one coming up."

Paredón looked at him sharply. "You think so?"

"I think so." Dan held up another gold piece between his thumb and forefinger. "For four more piastres — in gold — I want to know how those rifles got to where they were found."

"But *naturalmente* they were found at your camp where you left them?"

"If we went into Camanche country to sell rifles," said Dan, "would we have left them in our camp while we moved on?"

"It does not seem a reasonable thing," Paredón admitted. "But the *ingleses* are not always reasonable."

"You never heard of an *ingles* going off and leaving two brand-new rifles for the Spanish to find, did you?"

"No, not that."

"Then," Dan said positively, "somebody planted them on us and told the lieutenant Borica where to look for them — or perhaps delivered them to him personally and paid him to arrest us."

Paredón shook his head slowly. "I have sorrow. Borica is in Tejas under the *comandante-inspector*, and I cannot . . ."

"You can find out," Dan insisted. "I'm not asking for evidence to use in court. I want to know for my personal knowledge."

"The courts are no more concerned, anyway, *señor*, for the case has gone to the king."

Dan continued to hold up the gold piece. "I still want to know."

Paredón considered. "It is in your mind, perhaps, that when you are released you will find this *hombre* who told Borica about the rifles, and you weel have a private settlement, no?"

"That is exactly what is in my mind — yes. I will give you this now, and another like it when you tell me the name of the man."

Paredón took it thoughtfully. "It may take a while, and I do not guarantee the information. It weel be only gossip."

"That is all right."

"*Bien, señor*."

178

Paredón inspected their irons daily for a week, but made no reference to the rifles. On the eighth day his white teeth flashed in the semi-gloom of the cell. "I have received a certain bit of information about the man who turned in the rifles, *señor*."

Dan had another gold piece in his fingers. "I'm listening," he said, "for a name."

"It is rumour, and I cannot answer for the truth of it, *señor*. I can only repeat what is said."

"That's good enough — if there's a name."

"*Un hombre* from Natchitoches, it is said, weesh to get you in prison. Is said he paid *cien pesos* — a hundred dollars — for your arrest."

Dan waited, holding the coin where the dim light reflected from it dully.

"Hees name is Juan Meserbi, they say. Myself, I do not know, *señor*."

Dan gave him the gold piece.

"You understand it is no good to tell this thing in court, for the case . . ."

"Has gone to Madrid."

"*Sí señor*."

Dan sat cross-legged on the floor after Paredón had gone, and Menard looked down at him as soon as he had slipped off his leg-irons. "You don't tell me, I don' worry."

Dan got up. "All right, I can worry enough for both of us."

"Is a strange thing, though."

"Did you say we could get out of here at night?"

"I have been told."

"How much?"

"Half a peso for the two of us."

Dan nodded. "Let's prowl."

Sometime after dark the guard, who carried a short sword from his belt, paused at their door. "*Ahora, señores.*"

The door swung open, and Menard gave him a coin.

"*¡Silencio!*" the guard warned. "Through the little room at the side of the big cage."

They walked across the cobblestones and through a small sentry-house. They were out of the *juzgado* for the night. The only requirement, Menard said, was that they return before daylight.

The streets were wet and there was some rain still coming down. Three blocks away they rounded a corner and came to the centre of Méjico. The *tortilleras* sat on all sides, mostly older women, smoking their incessant *cigarros*, guarding a small pot of *guisado* or *chile colorado* which was kept warm by a tiny charcoal fire, and displaying within reach a stack of *tortillas* to serve as eating utensils and bread. Some of the *viejas* sat in silent contemplation, not seeming to care whether they sold their wares or not, but smoking incessantly, while others called out their products in high but not unmusical voices.

Small bare-footed boys with blazing torches ran before lumbering coaches, while *cargadores* or porters stood at the street corners to carry passengers across the flooded streets on their backs.

The *pordioseros* — a grade higher than *léperos* — were on every hand, sometimes walking, sometimes

180

sitting as if crippled and extending supplicating arms, calling, "*Por Dios, señor. Por Dios.*"

Dan shouldered his way through the crowds, a head taller than most of them, and the *poblanas* — the lower-class women — looked up at him with sparkling eyes and friendly smiles. They wore red petticoats, skimpy white blouses, and flowered *rebosos* on their black hair. Always without stockings but never without *cigarros*, they showed small feet and shapely ankles as they crossed the gutters and made their way to the *fandangos*.

Every three or four doors was a *pulque* shop, and from these came the twanging of guitars and the high, smooth tones of the *cantadores* singing about *pulque* and love unrequited.

"The women," said Menard, "look verr', verr' nice."

"Look out for a husband or a lover who would stick a knife through your ribs," Dan advised, pushing ahead.

Menard looked up. "Sometimes I weesh you wouldn' be so practical. You'd have more fun."

Dan looked down. "Sometimes I wish that myself."

They went into a *pulquería*, a filthy place crowded with men and women, sitting, standing, chattering. A man wearing over his upper body a sort of sack without sleeves looked up at them. Menard nodded, and the fat man poured two big green tumblers of *pulque*. "*Siéntense VV.*," he told them, and they found a table.

"*¿Son VV. ingleses* or *yanqués?*" the fat man asked, taking their money.

"English or Yankee?" repeated Dan. "What's the difference? They're all the same."

The man bent down. His breath reeked of *pulque*. "Are you two from the Acordada?"

"What if we are?" asked Dan.

"Is a nice prison — the Acordada — no?"

Dan frowned. "For a prison — yes."

"What's bad about it? You can go out at night. You can have company — and your board is paid by the king."

Dan looked at him. "I don't understand why."

"But why not?" He raised his eyebrows. "We all have to live. How would the guards buy *pulque* if they could not collect a few pesos from the prisoners?"

Dan shook his head. "It's a strange way of doing business."

The fat man shrugged. "*Es cosa de Méjico*. But all prisons in Méjico are not so comfortable, *señor*."

Menard emptied his glass.

"More of the delicious nectar, *señor*?"

Menard said, "Drink up, *amigo*."

Dan emptied his glass. Maybe the stuff would taste good if he drunk enough of it.

The fat man came back. "Have you then heard the news about the English colonies, *señores*?"

Dan came alert. "Is that why you asked if we were *yanqués* or *ingleses*?"

"*Sí, señor*."

Dan threw a coin on the table. "*¿Qué novedades?*"

He pocketed the coin. "The colonies have organised themselves into states, and there is much fighting."

"Fighting?"

"War, *señor*. But do not get up. Sit here and drink your fill of this lovely *pulque*."

Dan said softly, "States!"

Menard turned up his glass and handed it back to the fat man. "It's vile tasting, but bring us some more."

The fat man grinned. "A fine war!" he declared. "*Muy grande*. English and Indians against Yankees and French."

Menard raised his eyebrows after the man left. "That makes you and me allies."

"It does, for a fact — but it means something else: my friends and relatives are back in Maryland and Pennsylvania fighting the British."

"They can't win. They haven't got rifle works or powder factories. England . . ."

"That's what I'm thinking about," said Dan, staring at his glass. "How can they win without equipment, without money? The king has trained soldiers, great generals, all the money he needs."

"And if they lose?"

"They will be taken to England and executed as rebels."

"Well, there's nothing you can do."

"I can help!"

Menard tossed it down. "You're a good many thousand miles away. Anyway, what good is one man against an army?"

Dan slapped the table hard. "They're my people, my friends, my kin. I've got to get back and help them. Let's get out."

But a commotion arose when he stood up. Apparently the fat man had told others about him, for now a pretty young *poblana* with a glass of *pulque* in one hand and a *cigarro* in the other, tried to embrace him, crying, "*Viva los estados!*"

Dan got outside. He ignored the *poblanas* with their red or yellow petticoats, the *pordioseros* with their hideous disfigurements, for back in the colonies men were fighting a war. Now it was for a common cause, not Pennsylvania against Connecticut, but colonial against British and Indian. He thought of Indians and he thought of Wyoming Valley and his mother and sisters and the two children. He had been gone over two years now. He had found the rifles, but too late to help. Those rifles delivered to the colonists might have allayed the feeling against England and might have averted war. He had found them but it hadn't done him any good, for he had been trapped by them.

"Is not necessary you should be in such a hurry," said Menard. "The night is only starting."

"I've got to get back to Baltimore. I've got to find Meservy and wring his neck. I want to do my part of the fighting."

"You can't try to escape now. They would garrotte the guard who let us out."

Dan stared down at him. "We paid him to let us out."

"For half a peso," Menard said scornfully. "You never expected to buy your way out of a prison that cheap. He intend' only to let us out for the night, to have some amusement."

"He knew what he was doing!"

"Is not nice to die with a screw in the back of your neck, *mon ami*."

"It isn't nice to die with a Cayuga tomahawk in your brain, either, and those British officers would do everything possible to turn the Indians against the colonists. That would be their first move. They've played the Indians against us before."

"The British War Office . . ."

"Like all war offices, is concerned only with winning."

"Where you going now?"

"I've got to get out of here and get back to Pennsylvania. They need me."

"*Por Dios, señores, por Dios!*"

Dan threw a coin into the beggar's lap and kept his long strides.

"You better go back and start over again, then. You wouldn't want that poor devil of a Spaniard to lose his life over half a peso."

Dan slowed down. "You're right — but to-morrow is my last day here. That's a promise."

They went back to their cell and the guard locked the door, the rusty lock screeching as its parts moved. The guard resumed his pacing over the cobblestones, and the drone of mosquitoes drowned out the faint cries from the *pulquerías* and the *tortilleras*.

Dan paced the floor all night, while Menard slept peacefully.

When the blacksmith came in the morning, Dan said, "You better put those things on tight. I'm going to escape."

The blacksmith grinned. "*O no, señor,* you would not be such a fool. You are a *güero* — a fair-complexioned man. The Spanish women like you *mucho!* They bring you money so you can go out at night and buy *pulque* for other women. Is a very fine life, *señor.* Is not like Acupulco — and that is where they might send you if you try to escape."

"What's the matter with Acapulco?"

"Is a most mean *comandante* there — Villareal."

"I'll worry about that later," said Dan.

"He's *loco,*" said Menard. "Doesn't know when he's well off."

The *herrero* looked at the determination in Dan's face and put on smaller irons and set the rivets tight.

When Paredón came by that afternoon, Dan said, "You better look me over well, *capitán,* so some of your men will not be blamed if I escape."

Paredón shrugged. "I am very sorry, *señor.* I shall alert the guard."

Dan smiled. "Please do," he said.

"Is no laughing matter, *señor.* If a prisoner escapes, somebody's head will fall. I warn you, they will shoot to kill."

Dan grinned. "I am not an easy target," he said.

186

CHAPTER
EIGHTEEN

He did nothing for a week.

"It is a nice game you played," admitted Menard. "It was more than fair to put them on notice. But it hasn't been fair to *me*. I have to stay in every night."

"That won't last for long."

About midnight that night he put both their blankets against the iron-barred door and started a fire. The guard came running with a bucket of water. All over the Acordada the *lazarinos* were pacing the balconies and thronging the cobblestone outside to see what was going on. When the guard opened the door to take out the smoking remnants of the blankets, Dan walked out. He kept going to the sentry-house, went through it, and was outside. So far it had been too easy.

Vera Cruz was the port to make for, and he started in that direction, well knowing that a six-foot-four inch *güero* would leave signs that a blind mule could follow. He waited for the sun, and when it rose he walked east. He got out of the city of Méjico and attached himself to a mule train. He was with the *arrieros* for half a day when the officials stopped the train and asked about *un güero muy alto*. He started to run, but there was jungle on both sides of the road. It would take many men with machetes to get through that tangled growth. He heard rifles crack behind him, and slid to a stop, his hands over his head.

Paredón looked at him banefully. "You have tried to escape, you *yanqué*. I have told you not to do that. Now I'm going to give you another chance. Give me your word you will not run away, and I will not bother you."

"It's a good offer," said Dan, "but I'm not buying."

"You mean you're not promis'?"

"That's right."

Paredón seemed astonished. "You know what that means — no rights, no privileges?"

"I know."

"Don't you feel a little bit sad for all those pretty little *poblanas*, all lonesome for a *güero muy alto*?" asked Menard that night.

Dan gazed from the cell at the triple summit of Ixtaccihuatl; the Spanish called it "*la mujer gorda* — the fat woman."

Menard blew a kiss with his fingers. "Your Sarah must be *mucha mujer*, to merit such faithfulness."

"She is," Dan said broodingly, but he wasn't sure.

Two nights later he forced the lock and escaped again, but they caught him eight blocks from the Acordada. This time Paredón did not take it lightly. "Maybe you would like Acapulco better." He frowned. "But I will try again. If you have all this energy to escape, you have enough energy to work on the roads," he said. "You will go out with the chain gang every morning, and I assure you when night comes you will be glad to sleep."

The work on the road wasn't hard, but carrying the chain all day was, as the captain had assured him, a task to keep him weary, for it weighed some fifteen pounds, and it was never removed. He worked from sun-up to sundown, and tried to fill up on *guisado* and *tortillas*, and sometimes *chile* rich with heavy black beans.

A huge mulatto, six-feet-six and with shoulders as wide as a barn door, also carried a log chain and worked sulkily, with the guards seemingly almost afraid to say anything to him.

On the sixth day Dan escaped from the chain gang. He got into the jungle before he was noticed, and lay there all day, tormented by mosquitoes and gnats. Then the big mulatto found him and hauled him out with one hand.

Paredón was angry about that. He shouted at Dan. "*¡Mentecato!* Fool! I will teach you to play games with the Spanish army." He pounded the table with his sword. "Within one week, *señor*, you will beg to be left in your cell. I promise!"

Dan found out the next day what the punishment was to be. He went out on the road, carrying his chain. Then he and the mulatto were fastened together by another eight-foot length of chain, and set to work.

It was difficult, for they would have to work together. And in less than an hour Dan found that the mulatto had no intention of working with him. Dan was stooped over picking up a stone when the mulatto jerked his feet out from under him. Dan came up, his hands and knees bleeding from the corrosive action of the dirt and gravel on the roadway.

The mulatto laughed, and Dan hurled himself at him. The mulatto went down, but came up in a rage, his big black hands reaching for Dan's throat. But Dan stood off, punishing him with his fists, backing up enough to jerk the chain and pull him off balance.

The mulatto bared his teeth like a wild animal, and rushed at Dan. He got Dan in a bear hug, but Dan pounded him in the kidneys with both fists. The mulatto had to drop back. Dan jerked the chain and pulled his legs out from under him. The black went down, skinning his buttocks, and Dan dropped on him, pinning both arms.

The guards, seeing that Dan was winning, came up to separate them, and they spent the rest of the day in silence. Dan was alert, watching for trouble, but the mulatto had to think it over.

Menard said that night when they were stretched out on the floor, "You take good care of *Negrogrande, mon ami*, but you must know he is not through with you."

"All right with me. If he can stand the punishment, I can deliver it."

"It is a serious thing," Menard insisted. "It is told among the prisoners that the mulatto has been promised his freedom if he beats you into subjection."

"I figure that will take some doing," Dan said easily. "I took his measure to-day."

"He's a big man and ver' strong, and Paredón has offered to set him free if he will make you behave."

Dan smiled in the dark. "So the *capitán* has put me down as an irreconcilable."

"Whatever he calls you, be sure it isn't good."

Dan was satisfied with that. He'd never seen, nor did he expect to see, the man who could make him knuckle down. He wondered if the mulatto, suffering with a split nose, would be so eager to start the fight again the next day.

He was due for a surprise. The mulatto seemed in a maliciously good humour when they were chained together, and Dan looked for Menard but found out nothing from the worried look on the Frenchman's face.

He found out more an hour later. Their being chained together required them both to work in unison, and for a while this went along. But presently Dan, carrying a rock to surface the road, came suddenly to the end of the chain and almost dropped the rock on his foot. He stared at it for a second; then he turned to the mulatto. The big black, standing with huge legs braced wide apart, was grinning . . . and holding a short bull whip.

Dan hesitated, then started for him. The whip cut a welt across his back. Dan stopped, then got his breath and went on. The whip wrapped itself around his head, and the snapper barely missed his left eye. He closed with the mulatto, but the black pushed Dan back, the whip cut him again and again, wrapping around his shoulders, his torso, his legs.

Dan stood for a moment, gathering a great hatred. His muscles tensed and he took a step towards the mulatto. But he felt the unmistakable pressure of a rifle muzzle in his back. "*¡Cuidado, burro!*"

Burro — jackass! Dan whirled. The whip cut across his shoulders but he paid no attention. "*¿Qué hace V?*"

"We have orders from the *capitán*," said the guard. "You are a dangerous man, and so you will not be permitted to assault a fellow prisoner."

"He's cutting me to pieces with a whip!" shouted Dan.

The guard shrugged. "We have our orders, *señor*."

Dan's jaws hardened and his eyes narrowed. "Then this Jamaican is to beat me until I beg for mercy."

"If you show repentance . . ."

"Not me," said Dan. "You can tell the captain for me that a *colonialista* will never beg. Let him use the whip." He stared at the mulatto as the leather descended. "You will pay for every lash," he warned.

Negrogrande grinned and snapped the whip back into position . . .

By night Dan's back was cut to ribbons, and the lower part of his body was sticky with blood, but he walked to his cell — stiffly as he passed the sentry-house.

After dark two *poblanas* bribed the sentry and crept into the cell, mothering him with soft words and soothing ointments.

"The first time," Menard said enviously, "that I ever knew any good to come of a whipping."

They were still there just before daybreak. "*¿Cómo está V.?*" asked one.

192

Dan smiled. "*Muy pícaro*," he said. "Up to snuff."

The next day the mulatto had the whip again. The first stroke of the leather across Dan's tender back was like the slow course of a smoking branding-iron, and Dan thought for a moment he would faint, but he stood it and waited for the second, eyes closed. He heard the whistle of the whip through the air, and felt the leather curl around his back. He stood there for a long time, until all feeling was gone save the dripping of blood down his legs, and still he could hear the leather thud against his flesh. Presently he opened his eyes again. The mulatto was still swinging the whip. Two guards were standing ten feet from Dan, their rifles pointed at him. Dan jeered at the mulatto. "What's happened to your strength, you black bastard?"

The mulatto renewed the fury of his whipping, but again it lost its ferociousness, and again Dan, barely able to support himself on all-fours, jeered him. "No guts!" he said.

"You're afraid of me. You're afraid of what I'll do to you." He tried to grin. "And I'll do it. I'll give you back two for every one you give me. Whip away, *mestizo*, and waste your strength. You'll need it later."

When they stopped for dinner, Dan was too sick to eat. But when the guards prodded him, he was up again.

The mulatto soon made another excuse to use the whip, as Dan expected. But he tired. His blows lost effectiveness, and finally Dan seized the whip and jerked it out of the mulatto's hands. He wrapped his fingers around the loaded butt and began to whip the mulatto.

This was a new situation for the guards, and they did not know how to handle it. Dan soon had the mulatto on his knees, and he used the whip to rip the man's back apart from every direction.

That night the *poblanas* were there and brought a wrinkled old *curandera* with baskets of strange herbs. Their gentle hands were soothing to his macerated flesh, while he had the satisfaction of hearing the mulatto, across the patio, groaning in his sleep.

The next morning the mulatto started in vigorously, this time obviously determined to end this strange contest, but again, when the black faltered, Dan seized the whip and applied it to the mulatto. The guards, with their rifle muzzles in his stomach, forced him to give the whip back to the mulatto.

The black used it a dozen times, but again his arms lost their strength, and again Dan seized it and laid on a score of flesh-ripping cuts before he lost it. This was repeated the fourth day, but each time the mulatto got the whip he held it for a shorter time.

The guards stood around somewhat uneasily, with their rifles raised, but Dan kept the mulatto as a cover. The mulatto got up again, and Dan curled the leather around his back. Dan himself had never felt stronger. He continued to apply the whip until the mulatto fell on his knees, rolled his eyes and prayed:

"Forgive me, boss. Please forgive me. Don' whip no mo', suh. Ah is almost kilt."

194

Dan took a look at him. The mulatto was as mutilated as he was. Dan threw down the whip and said, "You better get up. We've got work to do."

That evening Menard said, "You are an unbelievable man." He shook his head. "The prisoners were betting five to one the mulatto would kill you."

Dan lay on his stomach while the *poblanas* and the *curandera* worked on him. "How much did you make?" he asked.

"To tell truth," said Menard, "I am unable to make any bets the last two days, but here" — he held out a double handful of gold coins — "I have collect' about six hundred pesos. Is half yours."

"Count it out," said Dan. "It's the hardest three hundred I ever earned, but it's money and it will buy things for us."

"*Tal vez* you will take us to the *pulquería* when you are well, *sí?*" asked a *poblana*.

"If anybody has earned it," Dan said, "you girls have. You are all *muchíssima simpática*."

Menard grunted. "You learn Spanish pretty fast, eh? And no sleeping dictionary, either."

"We aren't out of prison yet," said Dan. "There's a lot to look forward to."

There was more than he knew. At midnight they were called to the office of the captain. "You have made yourself very difficult to handle in this prison, *yanqué*," he said.

Dan, carrying the log chain, felt more invincible than he had ever felt in his life. "I will continue to do it until you turn me loose."

"We have ways of making a prisoner more tractable, señor."

"You tried one," Dan reminded him, "but it didn't work."

"There are other ways — many others."

"You didn't call us here to tell us that. Anyway, Menard had no part of this. He didn't do any whipping."

Paredón sighed. "I could almost envy you those scars on your back, señor. There are few men living with such mementos."

"By which," Dan said, "I suppose you are getting ready to give me some more mementos."

"Not I exactly," said Paredón. "You have insult' the Spanish colonial government, señor, the viceroy. This we cannot permit. It is not fitting that a miserable yanqué should make a laughing-stock of the viceroy."

"It isn't necessary, either. The Spanish colonial government is capable of making a fool of itself."

"You are quite unrepentant, señor?"

"The only thing I'm sorry for," Dan said, "is the fact that you made me beat up the mulatto"

"He lost nothing," Paredón observed. "He would have his freedom if he had succeeded."

"Then we get *our* freedom, I suppose," Dan said sarcastically.

"I am afraid that does not follow, señor. I could find it in my heart, perhaps, to admire such a brave man, but unfortunately the matter is out of my hands. Higher officers have taken an interest in your case."

"And that means what?"

"It means, *señor*, that you two will be sent to the prison at Acapulco, where there are more facilities for handling unruly prisoners, and perhaps a more experienced *administrador*."

CHAPTER
NINETEEN

They left in an hour on *burros* for Acapulco. It was a winding road over the mountains westward, and they rode all night with the shackles in place and the heavy chains across the bare backs of the *burros* before them. They bought tow-sacks to use as saddle blankets to keep the salt in the animals' sweat from galling their legs. They stopped in abode huts along the way and lived on *chile colorado* and tropical fruits until they reached Acapulco, Pacific port for all of Méjico. But they saw little of the lovely bay. They were taken to the huge old jail, and stood, still in their irons and chains, before the commander, Colonel Don Jesús María Villareal y García de Apodaca. Villareal was fair-skinned but black-haired, and wore a moustache that swept up at the ends. It was quite a luxuriant tonsorial adornment, but somehow out of place, though Dan could not quite decide what gave him that idea. The colonel sat behind a desk that concealed him from the chest down. His movements were quick and brisk, somehow inconsistent with the size of man he should have been.

"One English, one French, *no?*" he said in a silky voice.

"English," said Dan; "but not British."

The colonel's head popped up. "A *colonialista*, eh?"

"Yes."

Villareal examined a paper handed to him by one of the tall guards who flanked him on each side. "You are commit' to my prison by the *commandante* of Acordada as an incorrigible, *no*?"

"I'm the one," Dan said. "Menard had nothing to do with it."

"It is said you used a whip on *Negrogrande* and nearly killed him."

"I certainly did my best."

Villareal stiffened. "You do not sound repentant."

"You don't expect me to be, do you? They sent the big mulatto out to subdue me, and gave him a whip in the bargain. You want to see my back?"

"I'm not interested in your back."

"You asked what happened to *Negrogrande*?"

"You are mistaken," Villareal snapped. "I was merely commenting."

Dan didn't care. He had been kicked around for a long time, and he doubted that anything they had to threaten him with could deter him.

"Since I'm down as an incorrigible," he said, "you might as well know it wasn't the fault of the whip or of the man who used it."

Villareal glared at him. "Acapulco is known as a prison for the taming of incorrigibles. You may be sure we shall humble you, *señor*. You will beg for mercy before we are through. We have never failed."

"Maybe you've never had a Wyoming Valley Englishman."

He saw Villareal's eyes harden. He sucked in through his nostrils a breath that they heard across the room. For an instant it was deathly still. They were deep in the heart of the stone building, and for a moment there was, thought Dan, less sound than in a grave.

"*Abajo!*" The single word exploded from Villareal's mouth.

The two guards strode briskly from their places. Dan was not astonished when they were led down, first over flights of stone steps, then farther down over steps cut in dirt, until they must have been several floors below the surface.

"It looks to me like they're puttin' us away for keeps," said Menard.

"Villareal is jealous of his reputation."

"*¡Silencio!*" growled a guard.

"Shut up yourself!" said Dan, and was cracked across the buttocks with the stock of a rifle.

"They start soon," he remarked to Menard, and was aware of the temporary puzzlement that passed over the guard's face.

A rusty door swung open on screeching hinges. Dan was pushed inside before he could see anything in the dark. The door clanged shut, and Dan sat up from where he had fallen. "*Buenas noches,*" he said to Menard.

But the footsteps were far down the ancient corridor, and the light of the candle had already faded into the gloom. Presently he heard another screech and then a clang, and he knew Menard had been locked up.

He began to explore his prison, to feel the walls with his hands, for he had no light.

After half an hour he found that he was as near to being in a grave as he might expect to be and still be alive. His cell was about three feet by seven — just room enough for him to lie down to sleep on the floor — and without any furniture or fixture of any sort. The walls were made of rough stone and the floor was of dirt. He lay down to sleep, and found he could not even fling his arms out, so he lay on one side.

He thought the cell had not been occupied in a long time, for its only smell was mustiness, but since there were no sanitary facilities, he foresaw that it would stink like a hog-pen within a few days. That was providing, of course, that they gave him something to eat. From the looks of Villareal, that might be assuming quite a bit.

When the sun came up the next morning he discovered that he had a window — a slit in the stone about a foot long, four inches wide, and fifteen feet above the floor. How high it was above the ground on the outside he didn't know, for the prison was built on a mountainside, but he assumed the window was just above the ground. It didn't do him any good, anyway, for he had no way of getting up to it. The stone on the wall offered no projections that anything but a fly could cling to.

He could lie on his back, he could sit, he could stand . . . and that was all. At about noon two guards came down and shoved a wooden plate under the door. He

201

took it in and surveyed the contents; one piece of black bread and one chicken-head, cooked. A gourd of water was brought later, and he wondered when they would bring another meal.

They did not until the next day. Then he was famished and ate every tiny scrap of meat and sucked the bones. Later in the afternoon he tried to call Menard, but discovered that apparently he was in a section of the prison cut off from everybody else. He stood at the barred door and called, "¡Viva el rey!" but got no answer. He called Menard, but nobody replied. He finally made out a heavy oak door in the direction in which they had taken Menard on the first night.

The next day, when the guards brought his food, there was still only a chicken-head and a piece of bread and a gourd of water. He watched them come through a massive oak door and shut it behind them. They shoved his food under the iron bars and went out.

So he was in solitary confinement. They expected to break him that way. Villareal felt there was more than one way to skin a cat. Well, there was more than one way to resist, too. He would see who was the stronger, Villareal or Shankle. Could Villareal dish out more punishment than Shankle could absorb? It was an interesting speculation.

Each day when they brought him the food he broke a small piece out of the gourd and put it in a corner so he could count the days. He had about forty pesos left, mostly in gold, sewed in the soles of his moccasins, but he dared not use it until he had been there a while, for he knew that Villareal would be watching for something like that, and if they ever found that he had money they would not rest until they had all of it. And he did not think it would be loyal to the pretty little *poblanas*, who had given him the gold, to let Villareal find it.

So he marked off a day at a time until he had been there a month, walking up and down the seven feet of his cell, stretching himself, examining the walls, examining the door and its fastenings, staring at the tiny gleam of light that marked the very high window — for he could not see the sky itself.

He marked off another thirty days, and used a piece of gourd to make a mark high on the wall, where it would not be rubbed off. Then he pushed the bits of gourd into the passageway and started again. But one day, staring up, he saw motion on the wall near the very high window. At first he thought it was some kind of insect, for it was almost the colour of the stone-grey wall, and he froze for minutes until it moved. It came lower on the wall, and gradually, very gradually, he backed into position where he could see it better, and watched its slow progress down the stones.

Finally, when he could no longer endure the bending of his neck, he lay on his back with his head against the door, and was disappointed to see whatever it was run up the wall and vanish through the window.

He was sad over that, for in these two months he had heard no human sound and had seen nobody except the two guards who appeared for a moment each day with his bread and water and chicken-head. He had grown a long, curly blond beard, and he had lost a great deal of weight, so that he was thinner than ever and could put his own hands around his waist, but he was more hungry for companionship than he was for food. He had said no word to his guards. He would not give Villareal that satisfaction.

But the next day he was in position early and waited for whatever it was to appear on the wall. Presently it did — hardly more than a shadow, and he wondered if it was something he could make friends with.

It got half-way down the wall that day before it got scared and skittered back up and out through the window, and he saw then it was a lizard of some sort.

The third day it got to the floor and walked towards his foot, a timid thing standing high on tiny legs, with its triangular head held high, its tiny black beads of eyes more wary than the eyes of a deer.

The fourth day it climbed up his leg, and he lay with his head against the iron bars, afraid to move for fear of scaring it. It walked over his body, its head darting everywhere, before it skittered back up the wall.

The fifth day it climbed on to his body and stood on his chest, staring at his eyes. He blinked, and it disappeared. He could not find it again until it ran out through the window.

The sixth day it spent more time. It was about ten inches long from the tip of its triangular head to the end of its slim, mouse-like tail; it was white, but its body was so transparent that he could plainly see its bones. It snapped at a fly that buzzed by, and that gave him an idea. He caught a dozen flies, and the next day, when it came down, he had his hand extended, the flies lying in his palm. The lizard ate the flies and went back.

He had seen these in Querétaro, where the Spanish called them *quijas*, and so he named this one Quija. It came every day at about the same time. He fed it with flies, and taught it to sit up on its hind legs to eat them. He learned to move slowly in such a way as not to alarm it.

Two more months went by, and still there was no single word from the outside.

Then one day, after the guards had left his chicken-head, he heard an odd shuffling. It made chills run down his back, for it would come and stop, come and stop. He tried to imagine what it could be. He had once seen a bear with its hind quarters paralysed, that dragged itself with a similar sound, but surely no such animal would be loose in the prison of Acapulco. He thought of a giant snake, and measured the space under the door with his fingers. There was only five inches — not enough for him to slip through, even as thin as he was, but enough for a good-sized constrictor to come into his cell.

But why would a snake come into his cell? Would Villareal, tiring of losing the game, starve a snake and turn it loose down there in the bowels of the prison? And if so, where would he get a snake big enough to swallow a man? But he saw at once that it wouldn't need to swallow him. A big enough snake could kill him with constriction.

The shuffling came closer, and he saw the great oak door had been left ajar. He saw, too, a moving object on the floor.

It wasn't a snake. It wasn't a bear. Whatever it was, it looked like a human. The thing shuffled closer, one move at a time, like an inchworm, and finally he heard it croak, "¡Por Dios, señor! Por Dios!"

He relaxed. A beggar, a *pordiosero*. But what a beggar! The man had no arms. Hanging from a great strap around his neck was a thick leather pad that covered his chest, and on this he pushed himself along with his foot. But why didn't he walk? Dan wondered.

The *pordiosero* had only one leg, and no arms to handle a crutch, so he pushed himself along on his chest. How he had got down there, God alone knew, but there he was, and his hoarse croak, "¡Por Dios, señor!" was now at the iron-barred door.

Dan tossed him a peso. "But wait, *pobrecito. ¿Qué novedades hay?*"

"*El comandante* is very pleased that you are so quiet, señor. He says the *ingles* has gone crazy, and some day they will forget to bring his chicken-head."

"So he's pleased, eh?"

The beggar shrugged. Somehow, without arms, it was even more expressive. "I only know what I hear, señor."

"I have one more coin — a gold coin," Dan whispered. "I will buy a knife from you."

"A gold coin?" He seemed to consider. "*Por supuesto, señor.* Reach inside my shirt there."

It was a long, thin blade of good steel. Dan thrust it under his belt and gave the beggar a double-real.

"*Mil gracias, señor. Mil gracias.*"

"*De nada*. Think nothing of it — but forget that you have done this."

"I have no choice, *señor*. Villareal would have any other leg if he knew this."

"*¿Qué novedades más?*" Dan asked quickly.

"*¿Más?*" The beggar considered. "It is said the British are about to defeat the *colonialistas* in Nueva York. But that is news of no importance."

"Anything is news of importance, *hombre*. *Dírgame mas. Más*, I tell you. *¡Más!*"

"A very wealthy widow has inquired many times about you, *señor*."

"A wealthy widow?"

"*La señora* María Trinidad Velasco."

"Why is she asking about me?"

"She is young, *señor*, and very wealthy, as I say, and also very beautiful. *También*, she saw *un ingles muy alto* brought into Acapulco prison. She has asked about you?"

The beggar started to turn on his chest-plate, but Dan seized the bars and rattled the door. "Don't go yet! I haven't heard a human voice in four months. Don't go, I say. Tell me more about María Trinidad Velasco."

"She wished to know if you are still alive, *señor*."

"Tell her . . ." He knew what a beautiful Spanish widow would expect if she bribed him out of Acapulco prison. A man couldn't say, "Thank you, *señora*," and go his way. The Spanish women weren't like that. "Tell her," he said finally, "that the *ingles* is in fine health and excellent spirits, that one day he will come out of this prison and break Villareal's backbone with his two hands."

"¡Bravo! Br . . . caramba! Vámonos!"

He scuttled away on his one leg so fast that Dan could hardly believe it. He was behind the oak door when the two guards entered, and he got out of the open door silently by a simple process; he rolled. The guards were at the door, holding the candle high. They stared at Dan and he stared back, refusing to talk, because he knew they would not answer. There was one bright hope: the widow had given the beggar money to bribe his way into the prison. Some day, when it was possible, he would hear from her again.

In the meantime, his friend Quija saved him from insanity. He caught flies for the lizard, and waited every day for its arrival. If it was late, he trembled with fear. If it would not eat flies, he tried slavishly to please it with offerings of tiny bits of food saved from his chicken-head.

It was amazing how little a man had to have to live. He marked off eight more months, and it was a year. By his calculation it was now 1776. He was feverish to know about the fight for independence, but there was no way he could learn. Or was there?

When the guard next appeared with his chicken-head, he asked casually, "¿Qué hora es? What time is it?"

The guard looked at him stupidly. Then he opened his mouth wide and held the candle close. He had no tongue. So that was one of Villareal's tricks. Dan drew a deep breath and sank back into his corner. He used the knife to dig out a hole in the wall where he could secrete it if he should be searched. He saved the white dust and mixed it with saliva to form a paste and plug up the hole so the knife could not be seen. Then he rubbed it over with dirt until it was the same colour as the rocks. All this time Quija had come in almost every day. On the rare days when the lizard did not arrive he was frantic, wondering what had happened to it. Perhaps one of Villareal's guards had killed it with a boot.

In this way he marked off eleven more months, and it was now 1777. Then one day the lizard stopped coming.

A week went by and it did not appear. Dan was beside himself. He stood at the door and stared at the guard as he came and went, but he would not ask. He would not give Villareal the satisfaction of knowing what had sustained him.

But now there was nothing but the damp cell and the constant buzzing of the flies, and he grew to hate them. He set himself to catch them all, and every evening he pushed a neat little pile of flies under the door — but always there were more, and Quija did not return, so finally he knew that Villareal had won.

He thought about it for a week before he did anything. It was now a month and a half since Quija had stopped coming, and he had little hope that the lizard would return. His only slender link with life, his only companion, was gone, and Villareal had won. The only question was how to get the most out of it.

He decided on the food. The next day when the guard pushed his chicken-head under the door, Dan shouted, "Don't they have anything around here but chicken-heads? Who gets the legs and the wings? Do they feed those to the hogs?"

The guard looked at him and pointed to his ears. Dan sank back. So the man was deaf, too. The prison of Acapulco had not been overrated.

Dan thought about it all that day and night, and conceived a plan. For a month he kept the dry bones of the chicken-heads in his cell. They drew more flies, but he kept them just the same. Then one day, when the guard pushed the wooden plate under the door, Dan shouted: "*¡Hijo de cabrón!* I want food! More food!" He pointed to his mouth. The guard stared stupidly. Dan picked up the chicken-head and threw it into the guard's face. The guard seemed stupefied for an instant. Dan ran to the corner of his cell, scooped up the old chicken-heads in his arms, ran back to the door and began to pelt the guard with them. The guard dodged, put up his arms, then turned and ran for the door.

Dan sat down in a corner, trembling. Slowly he chewed the bread, which he had been careful to save, wondering what Villareal would do now.

He banked on the idea that Villareal wanted him to rebel so that he would have an excuse to punish him. He thought Villareal would be tired of this waiting game after more than two years. And he was right.

Within half an hour a squad of four soldiers with rifles at the ready came through the big oak door and ranged themselves outside of his cell. A fifth — some kind of officer, judging from the fact that he was better dressed — strode through behind them, advanced to the cell door, unlocked it, and uttered one contemptuous word: "*Vaya!*"

CHAPTER
TWENTY

Dan took a deep breath and walked out of the cell. He followed the soldiers through the oak doorway and up narrow dirt stairs. At first it was a little frightening not to have walls within the reach of either hand, but within a few minutes they were walking down a tall stone passageway, and then, before he realised, they were outside in the sunlight — the sunlight that for over two years he had seen only indirectly through that narrow slit. He blinked when it hit his eyes, and shook his head.

He had been watching for Villareal, but the *comandante* had not appeared. They took Dan to a square before the prison. Here were stocks and a gallows. On one side was a mountain that appeared to be almost vertical; on the other was a swamp.

Two soldiers lifted the upper boards of the stocks. Two others lifted him and swung his feet into the lower holes. It wasn't much of a lift, for he didn't weigh over a hundred pounds. He had been thin when he had been well fed; now his legs and arms were hardly more than cane stalks.

They slammed the middle board down on his ankles, the top board down on his wrists and neck. The commander of the guard put a chain through each post just above the top board, and padlocked them both. Now he was in front of the prison but facing away from it. Villareal could observe him without being observed by him. Well, a man couldn't have everything. At least there was fresh air and sunlight out here.

But a quarter of an hour later he discovered there was still more. With the commander barking orders, the four soldiers brought up a heavy wheel and hung it over his head. More barked orders. The soldiers backed away, two on each side.

Dan's chin now was against the board. The wheel had come from a big wagon; it was four feet high and had an iron tyre at least three inches wide. It began to press through the flesh at the back of his neck. He tried to get one hand free, but couldn't. If he could withdraw a hand, he saw he still couldn't reach the wheel, for his hand would be behind the stocks. Nor did he dare to turn his head sideways and present a new resting-place for the wheel, for he would never have enough strength in his neck to straighten his head against the weight. It was conceivable that the wheel could choke him to death if he turned his head.

At that time he heard the shuffling sound, and the armless, one-legged man came crawling on his leather breast-plate. "*¡Por Dios, señor!*"

"*¡Por Dios V. mismo! Por Dios* yourself?" said Dan through his teeth. "*¿Qué novedades hay?*"

The beggar took a better look at him, and pushed closer. "Is there something maybe I can do for you?"

Dan spoke with difficulty. "Tell the *señora* I am out of prison but not free."

He meant it as a grim joke, but the beggar's eyes softened a little and he said, "*Lo haré*. That I will do."

Then he spun on his breastplate and scuttled off.

In the next three hours he conceived an intense hatred for Villareal. The weight of the big wheel, always bearing on the same spot, seemed intolerable, and it was a question in his mind whether human bones could stand such pressure without relief.

The sun came around and beat down on his back, but no one offered him water. His mouth became like leather, and finally, towards sundown, he had no strength at all left in his neck, and all he could do was depend on the bone of his skull and chin to bear the burden. A strange thing was that, while the point of his chin was sore, his jawbone ached most at the hinge.

He didn't see how he could stand it another minute, but the hours went by and the parts of him that didn't hurt became a little numb. He began to think about escaping, but the knife was hidden in his cell.

As the sun set in the Pacific, the officer shouted orders and they took the wheel from his neck.

At first he thought his head would fly back through the board. Then they raised the stocks and, when he tried to straighten up, he fell backwards. They released his feet and started him for the prison. He remembered to get one last look at the lie of the land. Then the big doors opened and he was again in the high passageway. They took him back down to his cell and clanged the door shut on him, and he sat there in the dark, rubbing his bloody neck, trying to keep from screaming.

The next day the deaf-and-dumb man was back. He shoved the food under the door, and Dan sat back in a corner and watched it. The flies began buzzing around the chicken-head, and he sprang towards it, swearing at the flies, beating at them until he realised that he was bruising his hands against the iron bars. He took the chicken-head and the piece of bread and the gourd of water, pinched a piece out of the gourd and put it in the corner, then sat down to eat slowly and thoughtfully.

Could a man lose his sanity for lack of another human being to talk to? Could he be tortured into imbecility merely by shutting him off from the rest of the world?

His neck had begun to heal, and the chiggers were about forgotten, when one afternoon, four days later, he heard the familiar shuffle of the *pordiosero*.

"*¡Señor!*" the cripple whispered.

Dan came to the door. "*¿Qué novedades hay?*"

"The *señora* Velasco saw you in the stocks the other day. She wishes to talk to you. To-morrow," said the beggar, "the door will be unlocked. Wait until the moon is up. Go through the door to the left. Keep going until you come to a stairway. There is a guard in that passage, but he will be drunk. Take the first door to your right. The guard outside that door will not see you if you walk out. Go directly to the road and then towards the swamp. The *señora* will be waiting in a coach. *¡Buen suerte!*"

215

The cripple wheeled on his breastplate and started off, but Dan stopped him. "Here!" He tossed a silver coin through the door. The cripple caught it in his mouth, said "*Gracias*," and scuttled out.

Dan stood up and watched the big door close. After all, there were men in much worse shape than he was. He watched the tiny slit above him. He hadn't seen the moon in over two years. How could he be sure when it was up?

He took the knife out of its hiding place between the two stones. He realised that it would be something of a problem to secrete, but he didn't dare leave it, for this might turn out to be his chance to escape. It would be found at once if he put it at his waist. He had no hat or deerskin cap by this time, so he laid it in one moccasin, under the sole of his foot.

This called attention to his clothes — the buckskins he had worn when captured up on the Camanche plains. Now they were thick with gease and dirt, for in all the time at Acapulco he had had no water for washing. He had bought a new pair of moccasins in Méjico and, after coming to Acapulco, had saved them by going barefoot a good deal of the time in his cell, for he knew that, should he escape, footwear would be vital. He had tried to toughen his feet too, by bracing himself between the two side walls of his cell and walking up and down as far as his strength would allow.

He looked back up at the slit in the wall. It was on the north, and even if he could walk up the wall that far he could never see the moon. He sat for a while and

216

tried to reconstruct the hour of the moon's rising from the time he had been in the Wichita village. His count of the days he believed fairly accurate, but he realised that he did not know enough about the exact drift of the moon's appearance to predict when it would rise to-night.

That time was important. If he tried to leave before the moon arose, he might be shot; likewise if he waited until the moon went down.

He watched the tiny slot above and wished he could see the sky directly, but the wall was too thick. He could not tell a great deal of difference between night and day.

He thought it over. The *señora* would most likely arrange for him to leave the prison after Villareal. How long did Villareal stay?

He faced the fact that Villareal had done a good job of isolating him; with a deaf and dumb guard, he knew almost nothing of his surroundings except that he was somewhere in the bowels of the earth under Acapulco prison. And suppose there were clouds to-night, and the moon did not come out at all?

Well, he would have to figure it out. The chances were that Villareal would leave by eight or nine o'clock. The *señora* surely would not make arrangements for him to get away in the early morning hours when any departure would be most noticeable. Then the safest hour would be about ten o'clock. Yes, if she intended to wait in her carriage, that would be the time.

But not being able to see the stars, he could only guess at ten o'clock.

He must make a good impression on her, or Villareal might have him down here until the records were lost and he would rot.

He was reminded of his dirty clothes and his unwashed body. Perhaps *la señora* would think he had rotted already. His beard was down to his chest, and his hair was below his shoulders. With his six-feet-four of height, he must be a fierce-looking cuss.

Eventually he thought it must be ten o'clock, and he tried the lock on his cell door. It opened at his touch. It must have been done when they brought him back — and he hadn't even tried it since. Habit robbed a man of imagination and initiative. He went out quietly, fearing even the squeak of the hinges in the darkness. He left the door almost closed, and went to the left.

The big oak door moved at his touch, and he went through. Here there were more cells, and it seemed lighter. He heard a whisper, "Daniél!" and whirled.

"Menard!"

He sprang to the door, thrust his thin arm through the bars, shook hands with the Frenchman, felt his arm, his shoulder. "Menard, I'm glad to see you! It's been over two years!"

Menard was close against the bars. "Daniél, you're like a ghost! What have they been doing to you?"

"Nothing. Absolutely nothing."

"Have they give' you food?"

Dan shrugged. "Occasionally. What do they feed you?"

Menard snorted. "Two chicken wings and a piece of bread every day. But sometimes they take me outside, working in the swamps, building roads, making hats. Then I get extra food."

"I didn't know. I have not heard many human voices since I have been here."

"I tried to find out where you were, but nobody would tell me. They always say, "No savvy, no savvy.""

Dan was scanning the cell. It was a little larger than his, and he finally worked his way to the top. "The moon! You can see the moon!"

"Sure. What's so —?"

"It's up!" cried Dan.

"Not so loud, *mon ami*. The guard will be in on us."

Dan said fiercely, "I could break any guard in two with my bare hands."

"Good talk," Menard said practically, "but let us face facts. You are so thin that an Osage could not follow your footprints across a mud flat."

"I've alive."

"What are you doing now — escaping?"

"A widow — Velasco, the name is — arranged for me to get away for the night."

"Velasco?" Menard's voice arose. "She can buy anything in Acapulco but Villareal, and he would lick her feet if she would let him."

"What is she like?"

"I have seen her pass the prison." Menard's voice got that far-away sound that told Dan more than anything he could say. "She is beautiful, *mon ami*, ravishing, and she is a woman. But you, of course, are promised to that belle of Baltimore."

Dan felt uncomfortable for a moment. "You remembered that?"

"I remember it. You remember it. Has Sarah remembered it? I doubt it verr' mooch. At any rate, the golden-haired Sarah is in Baltimore while you and I are in Acapulco. And remember more; *la señora* can get us out of this filthy hole if you are nice to her."

"I can do that."

"H'm." Menard considered. "I theenk I have use' the wrong word. A lovely, wealthy widow does not release a man from the foul depths of a Spanish *juzgado* because he is lonesome for the moon. It might be, if you are a little *affectionate* towards her, you will get to see the sun . . . and don't forget I'm here too."

Dan hated to leave, for, except with the *pordiosero*, it was the first conversation he had had in a very long time, and even his own words sounded strange to him. But he'd better get out while he could. The moon might set. The guard might change. The *señora* might get tired of waiting.

"Whatever you do," came Menard's whisper, "keep your mouth shut about Sarah. Let the widow think anything she wants to think — just so we get out of this accursed rock pile."

"Two wings a day," Dan said softly. "You lucky Frenchman."

"Don't worry. If I know anything about beautiful women who arrange rendezvous with prisoners, you will eat to-night as you have not eaten in your whole life."

"I could hope so."

"And when you have partaken of the lady's hospitality, remember — she is a widow!"

"*Buenas noches*," Dan said.

He went up a dirt stairway and tried the door. It opened readily and quietly. He went outside without making a sound. This side of the prison was in bright moonlight — a huge pile of stone and mortar. He looked for the guard, who was thirty feet from the door, gazing at the swamp. He walked away quietly, turned as directed, and followed the road. A huge European-made carriage was waiting behind a team of eighteen-hand horses. He approached it from the rear, went to the side in shadow, and knocked on the door. It opened. "*Entra V., señor*," said a soft voice.

He liked the voice the moment he heard it. It was the voice of a woman, not a girl — and not a woman who had to proclaim it, either. Somehow he knew that the owner of this voice did not have to go to receptions and parties to prove her womanliness.

He got in, met by the fragrance of imported perfume, heady in its gentle sweetness. He sat down, aware that she was at the opposite end of the seat, and he was ill at ease because of his dirtiness, and not too sure even now that Villareal's guards would not come after him.

The driver's whip cracked. The big horses moved into their collars, and the heavy carriage began to lumber ahead, creaking and groaning.

The windows were covered with mosquito bar, and the dank vegetation smell of the swamp swept over them. It would seem that the prison was well guarded, for the dry stretches of the tropical swamp were perfect for bush-masters and coral snakes — if a man would get through the mosquitoes alive.

Not seeing the woman in the carriage with him, for she sat back in the dark, he had almost forgotten her in speculation on escape, when the carriage made a sharp turn, and they took a road through the swamp. This led to higher ground, and within a few minutes they were travelling on a smooth lane between rows of palm trees. The dank smell was replaced by the clean fragrance of jasmine.

The carriage turned again and took a winding road through well-kept grounds that lay picture-like in the flooding moonlight. They drove up a mountain slope for a quarter of a mile and stopped under a vine-covered arbour. "*Aquí, señor,*" said the soft voice.

A footman opened the door, and he got out. He turned to give her his arm, and she took it, but very lightly, not with a gesture of possession as Sarah had done.

He put the thought out of his mind.

He followed her through a hallway, into a large room lighted by candles. There she stopped and turned to face him. It was a richly furnished room filled with mahogany, laces, and linens, but it was not half as finely wrought as the woman herself.

222

She was about his age, maybe a year younger. She was small, the top of her head coming to his shoulder. But she was finely built and completely all-woman from the voluminous folds of her black lace dress to the creamy white mantilla that set off her jet-black hair. She wore a little spot of rouge high on each cheek and her lips were like ripe fruit. Her skin was ivory-tinted and clear.

He gasped, for it was a long time since he had been within touching distance of any woman, and it was a little too much, coming abruptly face to face with such a woman as the *señora*.

She made it easy for him. "You've been in the prison a long time. Won't you sit down?"

"I . . . *señora*, these clothes are not fit to sit in. I would not feel at home sitting on your floor in these clothes."

She smiled as if she understood. "What would you like first, after all these months in solitary confinement?"

"As soon as I've had a chance to look at you, ma'am, and perhaps touch you to see if you're real, I'd like a bath."

"I thought you would say that." She raised her head and gave orders in musical Spanish. An Indian-Spanish maid appeared. "Please to follow Anita, *señor*. She will help you with your bath."

"I don't need help, ma'am. All I need is water."

"Don't be so modest," she said. "Anita will bathe you as she would a child."

"I'm not a child, ma'am," he warned.

She seemed amused. "Get your bath. The water has been heating all day. Then hurry back. There is food, and there is much to talk about."

He took a step towards her. His long fingers closed on her firm forearm, and he breathed deeply. "Yes, ma'am."

She moved even a little closer and looked up at him, her black eyes like stars in the candlelight. "I am quite real, *señor*, and you are *muy alto*, as they have told me — but too thin." Her eyes glistened with tears. "That *perro* Villareal has starved you. Yes, I have heard," she went on. "I do not know the details, but I have heard him gloat in his drunkenness that he would break you. It has become a matter of great interest in Acapulco, and money has been wagered on the outcome."

"I'm surprised he hasn't tortured me, ma'am."

"Villareal is a very sensitive man, and a man of infinite patience. He would not want to be accused of taking advantage of his position. It appeals more to his vanity to do it this way."

He looked down at her. "You've just set him back ten years," he said.

"*Gracias.* Now, *señor*, to the bath. There is food — meat and fruit and wine, brandy, what you like. Please to hurry."

He hurried. While Anita poured bucketful after bucketful of steaming water into the wooden tub, he took off his dirty clothes and held them before him. Anita paid no attention. She made the water the temperature to suit her. Then she got a large cake of yellow soap and motioned him brusquely. "*En el aqua.*"

He stepped in. It was the most delicious feeling he could remember, the warm water along his legs, his body gently scrubbed, the warm, soapy odour. He closed his eyes and let Anita bathe him.

He heard her gasp at the scars on his back, but finally she finished with the soap suds. "*¡Arriba!*" she ordered.

He stood up and dried himself on a big towel. He started to put on his old clothes, but she stopped him. Long black broadcloth pantaloons with flared bottoms were lying on a chair, along with a red velvet waist. He put them on, and was astonished to find that they fitted him. A pair of loose sandals finished the job. He slipped his feet into them, got his dagger from his moccasins, put it at his waist, and went back into the parlour.

"Oh!" The *señora* came at him in a rush. "You are so *bonito, señor*. I did not know." She laughed. "Your nose shines like a small boy's."

He smiled. Both of his arms went around her, and he held her close for a moment. She looked up when he released her, her eyes watching his gravely. "Do you wish to eat now, *señor*?"

"I reckon I better, *señora*. I'm . . . sort of forgetting myself . . . with everything."

"It's good to forget yourself," she told him. "Now, what will you have — chicken, beef, mutton?"

"Not chicken, if you please. A little beef would look mighty good, though."

"You will have first a glass of brandy?"

"Fine."

They touched the glasses. The brandy was the colour of old, old whisky, and he tossed it down in a few gulps. She smiled and filled it again. "Sit back, *señor*. I have servants to do the work."

He sat back and tried to relax. His situation had changed considerably in a short time. She sat on a stool at his feet, her legs somehow concealed under her. "You would like a *puro*, no?"

He grinned. He hadn't even thought about tobacco for months. She gave him a Havana and held a candle so he could get a light.

"We will eat when you finish the *puro*," she said. "There is no hurry. You do not have to be back until daylight."

He ate beef until he thought he would split, and then sat back and drank more brandy. Soon he would be hungry again and would eat more. And always her eyes were before him like stars.

"Now tell me something," he said finally. "Why did you do all this? Villareal has hundreds of prisoners in that pile of rocks."

"But they are not so *güero* — so fair-complexioned. And it is known from here to Chihuahua that the *norte americano* is a *caballero* — a gentleman."

"My hair is as long as a goat's."

"I weel braid it for you."

"All right. Go ahead." He puffed on his second cigar.

She began to comb out his hair. "I have heard many stories about you, *señor*. They say the *inglés muy alto* is hidden away in a small cell at the very bottom of the prison, where he has nothing to do, no one to talk to but himself."

"You hear that?"

Her small hands were very deft with the comb. "It is true?"

"You can hear anything around a prison, *señora*."

He could see her arms flashing in smooth, quick movements. He felt the heavy braid take shape. She turned her head to one side, eyeing him, then put her hands at his back to turn him to face her. But she screamed a little and looked at him in horror. "Your back, *señor*! The scars!

"That's nothing," he assured her. "I had those before I came here."

"They were terribly cruel to you." She pulled him back until his head was in her lap. "*¡Pobrecito!*" She rocked his head in her arms and murmured softly over and over, "*¡Pobrecito!*" She rocked his head in her arms and murmured softly over and over, "*¡Pobrecito! ¡Pobrecito!*"

CHAPTER
TWENTY-ONE

He ate again, and she was delighted. "I have never seen a man eat so much in one night," she said.

"You haven't often seen a man who had so much eating to make up for."

He had another glass of brandy, and finally sat back, satisfied. It was one of the best feelings he had had in a long time. He looked at Trinidad. It was three o'clock, and he would have to go back within half an hour. "What's the news," he asked suddenly, "about the revolution in New England?"

"They still fight, back and forth. Nobody wins, everybody loses. When did you hear last?"

"In the winter of '75, I think. They had begun fighting."

"Last year," she told him, "they have organise' the United States of America."

His eyes opened wider. "Good. And what else?"

"There is a declaration of independence, a republic, much fighting, always fighting." She pressed her small hands against her eyes.

"Where is the fighting?"

"In Carolina, Virginia, Nueva York, perhaps other places I do not know."

"What side are the Indians taking?"

"These things I do not know too well, *señor*, but it is said *el señor don* Enrique Hamilton, British *gobernador* of the North-west, has been ordered to start a reign of terror on the frontier. Indians are to be supplied with rifles and powder, and perhaps even offered a bounty on the scalps of the *colonialistas*. It is expect' to be a *muy* bloody thing."

He sat straight up. "Of course it will be! All the Indians in the country are up there, and every one is aching to bury his tomahawk in a white skull. All they ever needed was a little encouragement."

"You have people there, *señor*?"

"My mother and two sisters live right on the north-west frontier. They'll be in the middle of it."

"Then you must go. They need your help. You can go now!"

"No. Not now. I've got a friend in the prison."

"It is true he came here with you?"

"Yes. I saw him for the first time to-night as I was leaving."

"You would miss a chance to escape for him?"

"If I got away, Villareal would put him in my place." He shook his head. "I've got to figure a way for both of us to get out."

"You are not fearful of the safety of your loved ones in Pennsylvania?"

"I'm scared to death," he said. "I fought the Indians up there and I know what they're like. I know that Bloody Hamilton, too."

"Go back to the prison!" she said suddenly. "Go back and I will help you both to escape!"

He held her by the shoulders. "Why should you?"

She smiled up at him. "Because you are *inglés muy alto y muy güero, y tan bonito* I can hardly bear to see you leave."

"But you want something?" he guessed.

"My husband was an old man. He died five years ago, and since then many Spaniards have want' to marry me, because I have much money from my husband."

"Like Villareal?"

"Yes, Villareal is one. He would like my money."

"I think you are overlooking something, *señora*. You are *muy simpática también*."

For a moment it seemed her heart was pouring out of her eyes. "Do you theenk so?"

"A man would be a fool not to see that."

"You have make me very happy, *señor*."

He finished the brandy. "Why don't you want Villareal?"

She shuddered. "He is a beast. I loathe him."

"I have no love for him myself, but he's nice looking."

"He is a beast," she said emphatically. She got to her feet with the grace peculiar to Spanish women. She ran to a small silver box and came back with a handful of gold pieces. "Here are a hundred pesos — if something happens that we do not know. Listen to me."

"I'm listening." He was fascinated by her intensity.

"I have sell most of my land and cattle and send the money to Nueva Orleans. It is a Spanish colony. If I arrange for you to escape, you take me with you to that city. That is all I ask."

"That ought to be easy."

"Is easy," she said. "I will have a ship in Acapulco from China within two or three months. I will prepare a cargo to Nueva Orleans and arrange passage for three persons."

"You don't have to do this for me, *señora*. It's your ship. You could go by yourself."

"It is not easy for a woman to travel alone on such a long trip. Besides" — her small white hand lingered on his forearm — "perhaps I want to do this for you, *señor*."

"Because I am *inglés* and *muy simpático*."

"Because *you* think *I* am," she answered.

He started for the door. "*¡Un momento!*"

He stopped.

"You had better change back to your old clothes. Villareal would know."

He nodded and went to the kitchen. In a moment he was back.

"Could I have also thread and a needle?"

"*Seguro.*"

"*Mil gracias, señora*, for a thousand favours — food, brandy, cigars, a bath" — he looked down at her and smiled — "and you!"

"I'm so sorry — you must hurry."

It was worth a month in prison to see the glad light in her eyes. He got out quickly. The carriage was still waiting. He got in and it drove off at once.

231

When he left the carriage, he felt the knife at his waist as he started down the road. The carriage rumbled off. Only then he noticed that he had not changed back to his moccasins. He swore, but all he could do was throw his Spanish shoes into the swamp and proceed on bare feet.

It was just breaking light in the east when he slipped in the outer door. He went down the dirt steps to Menard's cell.

"What luck, *mon ami*?"

The question, coming out of the dark, almost frightened him, but only for a moment. "Very good," he whispered. "She's young, rich, and beautiful — and she will help us escape."

"What is the price? Do you have to marry her?"

Dan frowned in the dark. Marry? He hadn't really thought of that. "She asks us to take her to New Orleans."

Menard sighed. "That is long enough for even you."

"You forget —"

"Forget . . . Hell! Sarah is in Baltimore, while you and I are in the *juzgado* for four years now. And with Trinidad panting for you to take her in your arms . . ."

"She didn't say anything about that."

"Naturally not. She is a woman and you are a man. Words are not necessary in such a case."

"You think she wants me to marry her?"

"She wouldn't have to go to all this trouble to get a lover, would she?"

"Well, I —"

232

"Don't be a fool," Menard said harshly. "If you don't marry her, I will."

"It is getting light," said Dan. "She will arrange for us to escape as soon as her ship gets in from China."

"One month, three months, six months . . ."

"Are you complaining? I came back to my chicken-head a day because I didn't feel like leaving you to Villareal."

"You liar!" said Menard. "You came back because you're afraid of María Trinidad Velasco, because you asked a blonde empty-head in Baltimore to marry you — and she's probably got grandchildren by this time."

But Dan, his belly full for the first time in years, was not inclined to argue about anything. "Keep your eyes peeled," he said.

In mid-morning a guard came down and closed the big brass lock, and Dan said, "I will give you four pesos for two knives."

The guard eyed him sullenly. "*Bien*. Give me the money."

"Get me the knives first."

The guard was back three days later, and Dan gave him a gold piece. "Six pesos for two razors," he said.

"You have knives. Now you want razors."

"For six pesos."

"*Bien*." A few days later he brought the razors. "I cannot come down here any more. Villareal is suspicious. He is like a madman lately."

"All right. Forget these knives and I will forget that I paid you money for them."

He used the needle and thread to fashion a sling for the knives and razors on the inside of his buckskin pants, on the inner leg. Then he used the old knife to make new hiding-places to hide the sharp weapons, plugged up the holes, and sat back to count the days.

One month, two months, three months went by, and he began to be discouraged. The chicken-head he got each day was almost nothing. He had eaten more meat that one night with Trinidad than he had eaten in all his time in the Acapulco prison. After four months, he began to wonder if Trinidad had forgotten. Then one evening, five months after his visit to her and near the first of the year, something was pushed through the slit over his head and began to descend on a long piece of rawhide. Dan was waiting for it impatiently when it came within reach. It was a cow's bladder filled with liquid. He sniffed and smelled brandy. Too bad Menard wasn't there. He drank it all — over a pint — and was drunk for the first time for years. The liquor went into his empty stomach and his starved tissues and hit him so hard that he lay back on the floor, blissfully intoxicated.

It wasn't until the next morning that he thought to examine the bladder, and found the one word "*Mañana*" written on it.

He bounded up so fast that he got dizzy and ill, and lay down again until it passed off. Then he carefully rubbed the bladder against the floor until the word was obliterated. He got the two good knives and the two razors and put them in their slings in his pants. He got the old knife, which now was pretty dull and not much use for a fighting weapon, and put it in his belt. Then he sat down to wait. It might be minutes. It might be hours. And it was hard to control his excitement.

The hours before noon were long. He ate his chicken-head and his bread and controlled his impatience because there was nothing else to do. An hour later an officer came down the stone stairway accompanied by two soldiers. "It has been told to me that you know how to make gunpowder," he said slowly and carefully.

"*Seguro*," said Dan. "My friend Menard has made powder, too."

The officer spoke to one of the soldiers, who went back up the stairway and returned presently with a blacksmith. They unlocked the door, sent the blacksmith inside, and locked the door again. The blacksmith began to build up the fire in his forge.

Dan showed him a gold coin. "For you," he said quietly, "if you make the collars loose."

The blacksmith looked sad. "Is my sorrow, *señor*, but I cannot do it. Villareal would have me in the stocks. He is very unhappy about the *inglés muy alto* who will not complain."

Dan thought he detected resentment in the blacksmith's voice, and he guessed that nobody around the prison liked Villareal.

The blacksmith fastened the leg irons and hammered the rivets down hard. Then he riveted fifteen feet of chain to each collar.

"What is that for?" asked Dan. "To pull a wagon?"

"Is orders, *señor*. Orders from Villareal."

Dan thought it over. The junior officer would have to be in on the plot to let him escape, but Villareal was taking no chance. The blacksmith finished and picked up his forge. The officer said, "*Vámonos*," and Dan marched out of the cell. They went through the other oak door and waited for Menard's chains to be fastened.

"I will not be able to do much work to-day on one chicken-head," Dan said to the officer.

"I have no orders to give you more food," the officer said.

Menard came out, and Dan saw him in the light of day. Dan laughed. "You've got a beard down on your chest," he said, "and your hair is below your shoulders."

"Never mind," said Menard. "I am going to find a *muchacha simpática* to braid it for me."

Dan thought the officer's eyes widened, but he said nothing. They went up the steps to the outside. The officer spoke to the guard. The guard expostulated. The officer shrugged and the guard came over and patted Dan around the waist. He found the dagger, its point long blunted by digging into mortar, and held it up triumphantly. The officer glanced at it and smiled. The guard waved them on.

Now once again he was in the hot sun. He wrapped the heavy chains around his waist so that they would stay up. He had neither shoes nor hat, but Menard had his original pair of moccasins.

They started down a gravel road along the edge of the swamp. In half an hour his feet were bleeding; Menard's moccasins, now several years old, had fallen to pieces, and he, too, was barefoot. It had done Dan little good to try to toughen his feet. The gravel under his tender skin was like walking on hot cinders. Then they came to a two-wheeled cart, and the officer stopped them and handed out bread and dried meat and parched corn from the cart.

Dan motioned Menard to move a little to one side, and they sat in the shade of the cart. He said in English, "There is high ground on the west, swamp on the east. When they start again, I will give a signal. You go to the west. I will go to the east, and we will meet on the high ground after dark."

Menard nodded. He was a wild-looking creature, Dan thought, with long black beard, tangled hair to his shoulders, scabby face, and clothes — little more than rags of buckskin — that covered a body like a skeleton. Menard, too, had two long chains fastened to his legs, and had wrapped them around his waist to facilitate walking. He was now barefooted, and his tender feet, also, were bleeding from the corrosive action of the gravel.

A call rang out from the officer: "*Vámonos.*" It sounded absentminded, Dan thought; perhaps the officer was thinking of a big house in town where a man could be entertained by a lovely woman.

Dan edged towards the east. The little squad began to march, but Dan held back and pretended to be picking a thorn out of his foot. He passed one knife and one razor to Menard. One of the soldiers looked back and asked sharply, "*¿Qué hay?*"

237

The officer, now undoubtedly a party to the projected escape, ordered him to come along. Menard had already pushed the knife and the razor under his waistband, and now he looked at Dan.

Dan moved a little, and the cart was between him and all the squad except for the one who was coming back. Dan balanced on one foot, holding his other foot across his knee. The soldier came around the cart. Dan straightened up and sank his dagger in the man's body about the navel.

Menard leaped head first into the dense tangle of tropical vines and brush at the west side of the road. A shot sounded, but Menard was already in cover and out of sight. In the meantime, Dan, under cover of the cart and the confusion, dived for the swamp in the east side.

Shouts came from the officer and the soldiers — a few aimless shots. Meantime Dan had got into the warm water, waist-deep, and was moving among the lily pads and reeds with only his head out of water. At first he crawled on his stomach, but the water became deeper, and he could walk. He avoided a big Mexican moccasin stretched out on a dead limb, and went to the opposite side of the lane through the swamp. There he crouched in shallower water. The Spanish soldiers ran up and down the road, pretending to look for him, and occasionally a bullet whistled over the swamp. The sun had been warm and good, but now a cloud came across it, and almost immediately mosquitoes arose in hordes and settled on his face and head and his bare hands. He slapped at them in desperation, but in a moment the backs of his hands were covered with blood — and he had to be careful of sounds. Then the sun came out again, and he breathed in thankfulness.

The soldiers went back some distance along the road, perhaps on orders from the officer, and Dan made his way towards the cart to see if there was any food left in it. He found no food but he did find a dead guard with a nasty knife cut in his belly. Dan was sorry about that, but he wasted no time taking the guard's shoes and slinking back into the swamp.

Towards dark the soldiers gave up the hunt and went back to the prison. Dan, watching from a squatting position in the swamp, with his head in the middle of a clump of reeds, counted them carefully. Then he waited another half-hour, while the mosquitoes and gnats arose in great humming clouds and settled over him. By full dark he saw no indication of a sentinel. The soldiers had taken the body of their dead *compañero* back to the prison, and undoubtedly by this time Villareal was getting a full account of the escape.

Dan waded through the mud, beat his way through the sawgrass that left long gashes on his thighs, and avoided hummocks of dry earth, for on those he would be most likely to step on a snake or get into poisonous weeds. He stayed in the lanes of brown water until he reached the road. He climbed on to the gravel, soaked, muddy, and still pursued by such clouds of mosquitoes that they were constantly sucked into his nose as he breathed. He sat down long enough to put on the dead soldier's shoes. Then he went across the road and started up the mountainside. The heavy chains around his waist were dragging at his strength, but he could not stop. At a clear place in the forest he stopped for breath. He heard shouts, and looked back at the prison. Soldiers were gathering in the light of resin torches, and he saw them start up the road around the swamp.

When he got up, the pain in his feet was almost unbearable. Tender from years of non-use, they had developed blisters on his way up the mountain, and now sand was in his shoes and made the pain excruciating as the grains ground into the blistered places. He took off the shoes and went on, but that was worse. He replaced the shoes, but in no time there was more sand inside them and he had to take them off again.

He reached a level two thousand feet above the road, and watched the yellow torches move slowly as the soldiers marched back and forth, and heard occasional orders barked.

By morning he was opposite the prison, and, according to his calculations, Trinidad's *hacienda* was straight over the mountain top. He hid behind a clump of sumac bushes, where he could put his feet on grass fresh with dew. He got his knife and razor, and used the knife to strike nicks in the razor blade. Presently he had a fair imitation of a saw blade, and he began to saw at the chain next to his ankles.

An hour and a half later he tossed the heavy chains into the brush, careful to see that they were concealed, and started for the top of the mountain. He heard Menard nicking his own razor blade, and kept on up the mountain until he found him. Menard looked up and flinched when he saw Dan's face.

240

"How are your feet?" said Dan.

"Not so good, but I can still walk on them."

"Then get those chains off and let's move. They'll bring out the hounds this morning."

Menard was still sawing at the last chain when they heard the distant baying of the dogs. It floated up to them on the still morning air, and Menard began to move faster.

"Which side do you think they'll take?"

"Villareal would rather have me than you, I suppose, but he's going to have trouble finding my trail. He can tell where I went into the swamp, all right, but all that swamp water must have washed me clean. The dogs won't be able to tell where I came out. It won't be until they spread out up the mountain . . ."

"Let me know if they do. I can wrap the chain around my waist again."

"Keep sawing."

The dogs wandered along the road, but mostly they seemed to be concentrating on the swamp side. Menard stood up, dropping the chain and tossing away the razor. "Do we go over the mountain now?"

"Yes, but we'll have to be careful. Stay under cover."

It was mid-morning before the dogs hit on a trail, and by that time Dan and Menard were well up towards the summit. Some time later the dogs yapped in an excited chorus when they came to the place where Menard had thrown away his chains.

"We'll have to double back," said Dan. "They're going to overtake us."

Menard looked down at their bleeding feet. "They don't need hounds to trail us," he observed.

But Dan was studying the country ahead. "See that tall pine tree up there?"

"Yes."

"Take off your shirt, tear it in two, and wrap one piece on each foot. That will slow them down a little. Then up this tree."

"You got a ladder in your pocket?"

"The bark is rough. You can climb it with your fingers and toes."

Menard winced. "With my feet?"

"Either that — or have a dog's teeth in your rear end."

"I never thought," Menard grumbled as he sat down and took off his shirt, "that I would do these things to fool a beast like Villareal."

"There's a turkey-roost over here. Walk around under it until you get the odour thoroughly in your shirt."

Having impregnated the pieces of buckskin they were using as shoes, they climbed the tree, reached a high limb, and followed it over a small chasm, then dropped on to a rock shelf. About that time the dogs came into the *barranca* below and lost the track where they had sat down to wrap the shirts on their feet. The dogs began to mill. Some of them followed to the turkey-roost, others wandered aimlessly in the brush. An officer began to curse the soldiers. "Two men don't just disappear in thin air in daylight."

"No, *señor*," said the handler, "but we have the trail pretty soon now." But he did not sound very optimistic.

Dan and Menard, fifty feet above them, lay flattened out on the rocky shelf, watching through a clump of yucca.

Noon came and went. The soldiers ate and resumed their search, the dogs now beating through the surrounding area. "Let's hope they don't come up here," Menard said.

"Maybe you haven't noticed," Dan told him, "but there is no way up — nor any way down."

Menard frowned. "No way down?"

"If we had one of those chains," Dan said thoughtfully, "we could toss it over the limb of the pine tree."

Menard judged the distance. "It's not so far. You could stand on my shoulders."

In mid-afternoon the dogs finally gave up and the Mexicans went away, the officer voluble, the soldiers tactfully silent. When they were out of sight, Dan yawned. "I was afraid, with the sun beating down on us, they'd wind us from up here, but maybe the air moves up from the cut."

They stayed on the shelf until almost dark. They had heard the dogs yapping down the mountainside, but they had no way of knowing whether a couple of the soldiers might have stayed back to watch for them. As soon as it was dark, however, Dan got back to the tree limb. He took the buckskin from around his feet and tied the pieces end to end. He let it down to Menard, and presently they were back in the cut, and Dan was wrapping the skin around his feet. "Without them," he said, "I don't think I could put my feet on the ground."

It was three hours to the *hacienda*. They skirted it cautiously, anticipating dogs, but none barked.

Dan walked across the grass towards the light in the front windows. He stopped for a moment behind a *madroña* bush. "Something is wrong," he whispered to Menard.

"Everything is wrong," said Menard.

"I mean . . ." Dan stood straight and looked all around. "I don't think we'd better go running in there."

"With a woman smart enough to have the dogs locked up?"

"Other things could have happened," said Dan.

"If it's a trap," said Menard, "let's spring it. I haven't had my chicken wings to-day."

"All right. You stay here. I'm going up to have a look inside."

He walked across fifty yards of grass and crawled up to the windows on his belly. He raised himself slowly until he could look through the glass window.

Trinidad was sitting so that he saw her from the side. She was very beautiful, he thought, with her black hair and creamy skin. She was talking, but he could not distinguish the words. Her voice came to him like the trill of a lark. He moved forward to see whom she was talking to. Then he dodged back, thankful that candles did not shed much light through windows.

He returned to Menard by the *madroña* bush.

"You jumped like you was shot at," said Menard.

"It was time to jump," said Dan. "Do you know who is in there now?"

"No."

"Villareal."

CHAPTER
TWENTY-TWO

They stayed back in the shadows. "What can we do?" asked Menard.

"Nothing that I can see but wait. We've got to have Trinidad's help to get out of Acapulco."

"What do we do? Wait till he leaves?"

"That's the only answer I see."

They waited — one hour, two hours. Menard went up for a look, and reported that Trinidad and the *comandante* were still talking.

Finally, at almost midnight, there was activity in the house. They saw the man cross the room. A few minutes later a dark figure emerged from the carriage entrance and walked down the road.

"To the back." Dan whispered. "We'll go in through the kitchen."

It was remarkably quiet around the big *hacienda*. Probably Trinidad had not only locked up the dogs but had disposed of the servants also. They paused under a grape arbour but saw nothing disturbing. The only sounds were the droning of mosquitoes farther down the mountain, the chirruping of crickets, the scratching of a ocelot's claws somewhere on the bark of a tree.

Dan led the way to the rear door. He pushed it open and went inside.

It was dark inside, except for the glow of coals in the cook's fireplace. There was the moist feeling of a room in which there were large kettles of water simmering, and he felt reassured. He had not admitted it to himself, but in the back of his mind he had wondered if Trinidad had planned to trick him. He had seen no reason for it, but a man in a Spanish prison for four years learned to be suspicious of everybody. Now, however, with the water hot for them to bath, he knew she had awaited them as escaped men. He went through the big kitchen and into a hallway, recalling the plan of the house from the memory of that one night.

The hallway was dark. He went through another room and saw a rectangle of faint candlelight at the opposite side. He remembered to remove the buckskin slippers from his feet, and fold them both so the outer surfaces would be covered. Then he tiptoed towards the light on bare feet.

He was within the door before he saw Trinidad standing at a window, looking towards the outside. He stepped towards her, making no sound on the carpeted floor. But there was a sound behind him.

Trinidad whirled, her eyes large and filled with wild fright. She saw him, and amazement came over her face. She ran across the room, crying, "¡Pobrecito! ¡Pobrecito!"

But something pressed against his back. "Do not move, señor. It is a very sharp dagger, and you will observe that it is opposite your heart."

Dan froze, and Trinidad screamed.

"Walk to the centre of the room, señor, quietly. My guard will be back in a moment. I told him to go just out of sight."

Dan took a deep breath. So it had been a trap by Villareal. "Did you know this?" he asked Trinidad. For some reason it seemed the only important question.

She was sobbing. "No, I did not know. I thought he had gone."

"I suspected you would come here," Villareal said in his silky voice. "The señora is known to have entertained you before. Now, señor, out of the side door, if you please. You did not thank me for my hospitality. That is a gra . . ."

He stopped suddenly. Dan spun around. Menard had one half of his buckskin shirt around Villareal's throat and a knee in his back. Dan snatched the knife. "If you're going to choke him," he said, "you must not do it here, Menard. Where are your manners? Don't you know the dog might throw up on the floor?"

Menard released the pressure of the strangle a little. Dan searched Villareal quickly for another weapon. He found a pistol, which he kept. Then he stepped back, keeping the pistol pointed at Villareal's breastbone.

"Go and wait for the guard," he told Menard.

Menard went back.

Dan looked at Villareal, and a great deal was clear to him. For Villareal was a dwarf, barely four feet tall. From the chest up he looked like a man; sitting on a padded chair behind a desk, he would seem of normal size, but now, standing on the floor, he was like a child except for his wide moustache and his hawk-like nose with the sneering lines extending upward from it. Dan thought now he understood some of Villareal's hatred for a normal man, especially for a man who could take ill treatment without complaint.

Dan asked with contempt, "What do you say now?"

Villareal's eyes smouldered with hatred. "I will have you behind bars. I will put you in the stocks every day. I will put you to the whip. I will . . ."

Dan controlled himself. For over two years of privation and solitary confinement he would have broken a whole man in two — but this was no whole man. He swung his long arm and slapped Villareal on the side of the face. The slap sounded through the room, and Villareal sprawled across the floor from the power of it.

Menard came back in. "The guard is taken care of, but I have not kill' him. I have only tie' him up."

"Very kind of you," Dan said.

"And this *lépero* — this *cabrón* on the floor. It would please me to roll him in the henhouse along with the guard."

Dan chuckled. "You have a fine sense of fitness, Menard. For a Frenchman you are a very intelligent man. But let's find out how much this *medio hombre* knows."

"He suspects," said Trinidad, standing beside Dan, "that we are sailing on the *Carlos* to-morrow night."

"How did he find out?"

"He knows it is my ship, and he must have checked with the harbourmaster."

"Well, Villareal, it looks as if you've got a long time to spend in the chickenhouse."

Villareal got up. "*Inglés*, I will strip your skin from your body, finger by finger, arm by arm, a piece at a time."

Dan slapped him again, and Villareal went down again. "Too bad you're only a *medio hombre* — a half-man. Tie him up," he told Menard.

"How about one or two very small kicks?" asked Menard hopefully.

"I don't really care what you do with him, but it might reflect on the *señora*."

"But I shall be in Nueva Orleans with you, Dahn."

Dan caught his breath. The girl was talking too much. "Take him out."

Menard motioned Villareal to his feet, and got behind him with the knife. "*¡Adelante!*" he ordered.

"For a man who is so merciless, he shows remarkably little fight," Dan observed to Trinidad.

"I told you he is a beast." She had her arms around Dan. "*¡O pobrecito!* You are so badly bitten by mosquitoes. Your feet are cut to pieces on the rocks. Your face, your head . . ."

"Never mind me. What we've got to do now is get away from here. Since Villareal knows about the *Carlos* . . ."

She said quietly, "He does not know as much as he thinks, Dahn, *mía*. I have let him think we are leaving on the *Carlos* because he wanted to theenk so. But I have make different plans for us."

He looked down at her. This girl, this widow, this Trinidad was no helpless woman. A woman, yes, but by no means helpless. "What are the plans?" he asked.

"Last week I have sell the *hacienda*. It is the only thing of substance I had left in Méjico. This is not known to Villareal, but I told him we are leaving for Nueva Orleans so he will be sure to take steps to stop the *Carlos*, for he has court' me for many months, and he will never forgive me for helping his prisoners to escape."

"And . . ."

"There is also a smaller ship of mine, the sloop *Confidencia*, which has been in this harbour for some time. This ship has been given orders to leave with the tide in the morning. It is perhaps best you leave *Señor* Villareal in the chickenhouse while you get cleaned up and eat all the food you can. Anita is in the wine cellar and will help. The *Confidencia* is bound for New Granada, and since I have tell him I am going to Nueva Orleans, I do not think there will be trouble. *También*, the *capitán* is an old employee of my father's, and I do not think he will be of any use to Villareal. You and your friend, now, get cleaned up. Anita will bathe your feet and your poor face, and before daylight you two must be loaded in hogsheads and taken on board the *Confidencia*. I will come as a passenger, and so soon as we are out in the ocean, you can come out. We will touch at New Granada for clearance, and then go on to Nueva Orleans. Is a good plan, *no*?"

"It's more than good," he said, smiling. "It's wonderful . . . and so are you."

Menard came in. "The *comandante* is disposed of," he announced.

Three hours later, bathed, brandied, fed, smoked, and soothed with ointments, outfitted in new clothes, Dan and Menard were fastened into loosely fitted hogsheads and rumbled down the mountainside in a heavy wagon. Villareal and his man were still in the chickenhouse.

Dan heard the horses pull the wagon out over a quay. They stopped, and for a while there were voices, and presently only the slapping of water against the posts. Then Trinidad's clear voice sounded. He had expected it to be a relief, but for some reason it was much more than that, and he could not quite place it. He felt warmth and confidence from hearing her voice, and a deep satisfaction from the knowledge of her presence. He didn't mind when they turned the barrel on its side and rolled it aboard. He braced his arms and legs against the sides and thought no more about it until the barrel was turned on end and left him upside down.

He waited until he heard no voices or steps nearby, and then cautiously reversed himself so that his head was up.

He heard the captain giving orders and the ship begin to move. He could tell when they were out of the bay by the long swells, and a couple of hours later the barrel was picked up by two men and taken down a flight of steps. A little while later somebody began to knock off the upper hoop, and very soon he and Menard were standing with Trinidad in the captain's quarters.

"*Señor capitán, son mis amigos.*"

The captain was an old man, wrinkled and grey-haired.

"*Buenos días, señores,*" he said.

"*Me da tanto gusto de conocerle,*" said Dan.

"I will give you seamen's clothes," the captain said, "and you will make yourselves familiar with the work on shipboard so there will be no suspicions from the crew. *¿Estábien?*"

"Suits me," said Dan.

It took them five months to clear from New Granada, sail down the coast of South America and around the Horn, come up the Atlantic side, through the Antilles Sea, and into the Pass at the swampy wilderness that marked the Mississippi delta. Day after day Trinidad stood at the bow or at the stern, and Dan stood with her when he could.

"What are you going to do in Nueva Orleans?" he asked once.

She looked up at him. "I do not know. I cannot return to Méjico, for I have insult' Villareal and I would never dare to show my face in that country again." She drew the *reboso* closer around her black hair, and stared out at the sea. "What are you do' when you get home, Dahn?"

He liked the way she said his name, with a sort of lingering caress. But he reminded himself of his duties. "I'm going up to Wyoming Valley to fight Indians — if there are any *colonialistas* left alive," he said, frowning.

"Surely there will be many left."

"Your captain tells me it has not gone well with the United States."

"It cannot have gone too well with the British, for the armies are still fighting."

"Do you think there is any way we could get help from Spain?"

"I do not know. My understanding of politics is not very much."

He said, "You certainly took care of Villareal."

"But I am nearing a strange country, Dahn." She shivered from a touch of spray blown up by the wind. "I am beginning to be a little bit afraid, I theenk."

"There's nothing to be scared of," he said. "The captain says Spain is favourable to the colonies, and particularly so in New Orleans, so I don't think you'll have any trouble."

"But I am a woman without a man," she said. "It is not always easy for such a woman."

They sailed up the river, east around the crescent, and north to the mooring posts along the Spanish section. Having asked directions, Trinidad took them to a large cypress house near the Place d'Armes. They had dinner that night by candlelight. They had wine and brandy, and ate with silver tableware from fine dishes on heavy linen. Trinidad's host was a white-haired old Spaniard who walked with difficulty with a cane. His wife was old and slight and also white-haired. His name was Don Eustacio Ebanito, and his mind was very quick. "You are a *colonialista*, eh?"

"I am. Menard here is *francés*."

"You are all welcome. How is the war going?"

"I thought you might tell me, sir. I have not been home for five years."

Trinidad said quickly in Spanish, "He has been in prison at Acapulco under Villareal."

"Villareal!" Don Eustacio crossed himself. "Heaven absolve me for the bad thoughts I have of that emissary of Satan!"

Dan enjoyed the food. There was fish and fowl and beef, with many kinds of bread — none of the *tortillas* he had been so used to.

"And what part of the colonies do you come from, *señor?*"

"Wyoming Valley, in eastern Pennsylvania."

"Wyoming Valley?" The old man looked thoughtful. "I think I have heard something of that. *¿Mamá?*"

"It was the massacre," the old lady said.

Dan stiffened. "Massacre?"

"Now I recall," said Don Eustacio. "It is about a month now that the news came to this city."

"What news?" Dan demanded.

Don Eustacio studied him. "I hope none of your people have been hurt by this, *señor*. It is a very sad thing."

Dan's spine began to feel cold.

"It happened on the third of July. Eleven hundred British Tories and Indians of the Seneca and Cayuga tribes, under the British officer John Butler and the Mohawk chief Brant, massacred all the men and boys in Wyoming Valley."

"Men and boys!" Dan's voice almost failed him. "What of the women?"

"All those not killed were driven into the forest or turned over to the Indians."

Dan sat rigid for a moment, then began to slump in his chair.

"You are faint, then?" asked Trinidad, getting up.

"No." He waved her back. "No, I'm all right. I . . . it's a shock, that's all."

Trinidad eyed him curiously. "You perhaps had a wife or *corteja* — sweetheart — there?"

He shook his head heavily. "No. Only my mother and two sisters . . . and they had no man to help them. I left . . ." He could not finish.

Trinidad was up, pressing his head against her breast. "*¡Pobrecito!*" she said softly.

CHAPTER
TWENTY-THREE

The next day Dan and Menard went to see La Mathe's agent.

"La Mathe used to be the biggest trader through Natchitoches," said Dan. "I presume he is still trading?"

"As extensively as the various regulations allow."

"Do you know a man named John Meservy?"

"We know him — yes," said the agent.

"Do you know where he is now?"

"He is west somewhere. The last I heard he was at Natchitoches, but he is a very hard man to keep a finger on."

"He's still contrabanding rifles?"

The scholarly looking Frenchman studied Dan. "You know Meservy?"

"Well enough."

"He is not a man to change his ways. If you want to see him, I suggest you go to Natchitoches."

Dan spoke to Trinidad that afternoon. "I have to make a trip up the river. The man who is in a way responsible for much of the trouble, who diverted rifles that my people needed to fight the Indians, is there. I must have a talk with him."

"You want to kill him, then?"

"I want more than that!"

"But you do want that?"

Dan considered. "It would not be a hard thing to decide," he admitted.

"Then please be careful, Dahn."

"I will . . . and you will be here when I come back?"

"I will be here praying for you to come back."

"That's good enough," he said, and felt her shoulders alive and firm under his arm.

Two weeks later they were in Natchitoches, talking to La Mathe himself.

"Meservy?" the old Frenchman said. "Yes, I know him, and so does Mézières and so does Galvez. But no one can catch him."

"Catch him?"

"*Certainement.* Everybody in Louisiana knows about Meservy. For a few years he was satisfied with a trading licence from Natchitoches. He picked up rifles on the coast and took them on west. But recently he has become more open. He uses his passport for free entry to the Indian country. He sells them rifles, and accepts horses, mules, and slaves — which *we* cannot accept — in large quantities. He takes these up to the *contrabandista* camp at Arkansa Post, because De Mézières will not permit him to bring them through Natchitoches, and Teodoro de Croix, the new commandant-general of the Provincias Internas, has made it difficult to dispose of contraband along the coast."

"So Meservy is an out-and-out *contrabandista* now?"

La Mathe said, "There is little secret about it. He left the Camino Real at the Mexican River a few nights ago with three hundred and sixty horses and mules, and twenty-two Apache women."

"Going overland to Arkansa Post?"

"It would seem so."

"And De Mézières knows this?"

"What can he do? The Arkansa territory is not in his command."

"Maybe," said Dan, "we can do something."

They set off towards the Caddo villages, and then north-east. They passed through the mountainous country, down over the plains, and into the swampy country along the Arkansa.

"It's about the same time of year as when we came here in '73," said Dan.

"And you were looking for the same man. It is a big hunt you are on, *mon ami*."

"It is about over." Dan watched the north-east horizon. "Will Blundin be there, do you suppose?"

"They don't usually last that long at *El Cadrón*."

They followed the river down along the high bank on the south side, and came to the big oak tree under which the Osage children had been after the wild turkey. They sat their horses under the tree and called across the river. A man came out of the blockhouse, spoke to a squaw pounding corn in the top of a stump. She went inside a smaller cabin.

"Let's swim it," said Dan. He put his horse down the steep bank and into the water. They came out on the sand-tar. The horses shook themselves, but Dan took them on through the protected lagoon and rode out on the sandy shore. The square, energetic figure of Poeyfarré came down to meet them. "Menard!" he cried.

Menard jumped down, and they embraced each other.

"I t'ought you were dead a long time," said Poeyfarré.

"You know this *inglés*?"

"Sure." Poeyfarré shook hands. "You both looking good. You have had plenty to eat, yes?"

"We're getting along," said Dan.

"You both talk like Spaniards. Have you been in Méjico ever since you went to talk to the damn' Camanches?"

"Ontil lately," said Menard.

"And now you want what? You have no goods, no money?"

"Where's Blundin?" asked Menard.

"Blundin?" Poeyfarré looked regretful. "I have had to kill him a couple of years ago. We have an argument over some mules."

"You're running the camp, then?" asked Dan.

Poeyfarré's answer was wary. "*Oui*."

"We're looking for a man," said Dan.

"I am no policeman."

"Neither am I . . . but I want to see John Meservy."

"Meservy?" Poeyfarré's eyes were suddenly veiled.

"John Meservy. He's due here about now with a herd of animals and some slaves."

"I know nothing about . . ."

"I'm not trying to cut in on your business," said Dan. "This is a personal matter."

Poeyfarré studied him, obviously weighing all the factors. "A herd of animals," he repeated, "and some slaves?"

"It might be," Dan said slowly, "that you could get them all for nothing." He paused. "If not, then you will have a good horse for nothing."

Poeyfarré asked Menard. "You been with this man since you left the Wichita village?"

"*Oui.*"

"You think he's talking truth?"

"If he's not," said Menard, "he's fool' me bad."

Poeyfarré looked at Dan. "He came down the north side of the river," he said, "last night."

"Then," said Menard, "he's camped over on the prairie behind the swamp."

"Far as I know, but I warn you, if you're trying to get my business, I cut your liver out and feed it to the birds."

Dan laughed. He put one hand on Poeyfarré's shoulder. "After five years in Spanish prisons," he said, "there is nothing you can say to scare us."

"What prisons?"

"Three years at Acapulco under Villareal."

"I don' know," said Poeyfarré. "You both look healthy to me. I've heard about Villareal."

Dan stripped off his shirt and turned around.

Poeyfarré whistled oddly. "*Sacre bleu!* I argue no longer. Go settle your difficulty with Meservy, whatever it is."

"*Gracias*."

"You damn' Spaniard!" said Poeyfarré, grinning.

"Keep the shirt," said Dan. "If I don't need it, you will have an extra one!"

Poeyfarré shook his head, muttering as they rode off. "I'm not making a bet." He looked at Dan's long, lean frame, now almost black from the months at sea, at the flatless and easy movements of his muscles, at his back ridged with scars. "I am glad I am not have to fight you . . . but I'm not want' to fight Meservy either. He has kill' many men since the Wichita village."

They took the path through the swamp. It was mid-afternoon and the sun was strong and felt good on Dan's bare back. Then Menard exclaimed, "He's there!"

"Let me go first."

"You want the rifle?"

"No, I've still got the dagger. It is enough."

"It would be easier to shoot him."

"I didn't come to murder. If I have to kill him, it will be in a fair fight."

He rode out. The horses and mules were spread over the grass; half a dozen groups of squaws clustered on the prairie directly before him. Dan rode towards them.

A man rode to intercept him. A big man on a big black horse. Dan rode alongside him.

He looked at the squaws beyond Meservy — short, heavy-set, with straight black hair. And no little ones anywhere. "I hear you're in the slave business," Dan said.

"I'm not interested in what you hear," said Meservy. "What do you want?"

"Several things," said Dan. "I found out about the rifles, but I owe you something for planting them on me. See this back?" He turned it towards Meservy.

A rifle cracked, and Meservy swore. His smashed pistol dropped to the ground.

Dan grinned. "I thought you'd try that." He said without turning, "You're a good shot, Menard."

Meservy leaped from the saddle, a knife in his hand. Dan lunged towards him, and they fell between the horses.

Dan's horse snorted and moved away. They rolled on the ground. Meservy grunted, stabbing with the knife. Dan kept a long arm on Meservy's right wrist while he snaked his own knife from under his belt.

They strained at each other until finally they pushed apart and began to circle. Dan thought he saw an opening and darted in. Meservy side-stepped and swung the blade at his back.

Dan felt a thump as the hilt of the knife struck his body. For a moment he felt nothing, but he knew the blade was in there. He twisted away from Meservy, pulling the knife out of Meservy's hand.

Meservy started to circle again. Dan tried to raise his arm, but a muscle hit the knife blade and it felt like white fire across his back. Meservy was still circling, warily now, for he didn't quite know what to make of it. He had another knife in his hand, and Dan tried to raise his arm again but failed.

He was near Menard, still mounted. He backed up to him and shouted, "Take the knife! Take the knife!"

Menard reached down and flipped the knife out of his back. It cut across his nerves going out, and this time he wanted to scream. But he moved away from Menard and tried once more to raise his arm. This time he did it.

Meservy rushed him. Dan caught his wrist and began to slash with his own knife. He found the soft gristle just below Meservy's breastbone, and sank the knife in as far as it would go. Meservy still struggled. Dan pulled the knife out and sank it in a new place.

Meservy staggered. He fell forward. Dan jumped back to get out of his way. He watched him for minutes, with the entire camp silent, the squaws, now all standing, watching the man's body on the ground. Bumblebees were humming across the prairie, and a shadow crossed the ground and over Meservy's body.

Dan still wasn't sure. He put one knee in the small of Meservy's back and pulled Meservy's knife out of his hand. Only then was he sure, for Meservy's fingers were limp. Dan got up and rolled him over.

"He's dead," said Menard.

Dan looked in the wallet of Meservy's buckskin shirt and found half a dozen letters. He opened one and read it. "This is the other thing I wanted to find out," he told Menard. "The name of the man who was financing Meservy."

"It is there?"

"Plain as bear-sign on the kitchen floor. The man's name is Patrick Evers, and now I have to go back to

Baltimore, for this man is still there, and he is pretending to be a colonial but he is working for the British. If I get back in time, I can at least help our cause by exposing him."

Dan walked over and wiped the blood of his knife on Menard's saddle blanket. "How do I look at the back?" he asked.

"Bleeding some. Are you spitting any blood?"

"No."

"Then you're probably all right, long as he missed your lungs. Be sore for a while, though."

Dan put the knife back in his belt. "Let's go back and get my shirt," he said.

They stayed with Poeyfarré that night. "I am one damn' glad you have finish' that fellow," said Poeyfarré. "I have a keg of rye whisky to celebrate."

"Let's get at it," said Dan, "before my back starts hurting."

They traded the horses to Poeyfarré next day for a canoe and insisted on starting back at once.

It did not take long, with the current, and the exercise, Dan said, kept him from getting stiff.

They reached New Orleans and went to the house of Don Eustacio.

"¡Señor!" cried the old man.

"Su servidor," said Dan.

Trinidad came flying. She was all black eyes and black hair and creamy skin and red lips. Dan took her in his arms and kissed her. Her arms went around him and held him tight.

Menard groaned. "What a damn' fool *yanqué*! I can never guess what he is goin' to do."

Dan grinned. "Neither can I."

"What does this signify — all this love-making?"

"We're going to get married, of course."

Menard sighed. "I was afraid. Don Eustacio, don't you think we should have a drink of brandy for this happy occasion?"

"*Sí, señor.*" He clapped his hands. "Rafael!"

"Now that you said it," said Menard, hoisting his glass, "you might as well know: I asked about Sarah Radnor when we got to New Orleans, and found out she married a man named Thomas Warton and they've already got three children."

"You could have told him this," said Don Eustacio, pouring more brandy.

"No. I want' him to make up his own mind."

Dan was still holding Trinidad, and she was holding him, with her head snuggled against his shirt. "Oh, Dahn, I have the big *susto*. I was so scare' you would not come back."

He looked down at her and smiled, and kissed her again. With his lips only an inch from hers, he said softly, "*¡Pobrecita!*"